MW00782092

Seashells
and
Murder

BAREFOOT SLEUTH MYSTERIES

BOOK TWO

H.Y. HANNA

CONTENTS

AUTHOR'S NOTE:

The popular UK TV show: "The Great British Bake-Off" is known by a different name in America. It had its name changed to "The Great British Baking Show". Since this book follows American English and is primarily set in the U.S., I have decided to use the American name of the show in this story.

CHAPTER ONE

"So… how are you enjoying Florida?"

Ellie smiled at the distinguished-looking, elderly gentleman sitting opposite her, who had asked the question.

"Oh, it's been wonderful so far! You know, I've always wanted to visit the famous 'Sunshine State' and it was like a dream come true when Aunt Olive—" Ellie glanced at the spry woman in her sixties sitting at the table next to her, "—sent me a plane ticket out of the blue with an invitation to come and join her here in Tampa Bay! London is so dark, cold, and dreary at this time of the year, so it was heaven to be able to get away from all that and come to the warmth and sunshine!"

"And I hear that you're going to be with us over Christmas and New Year?"

"Yes! My first Christmas outside England. Of course," Ellie added, beaming, "being able to stay at your beautiful resort, Mr. Papadopoulos, is the icing on the cake." She gestured at the view of the huge pool and the beach beyond, visible from the open terrace where they were sitting. "I've seen postcards and photos of beach resorts with gorgeous white sand and swaying palm trees and dazzling blue swimming pools and cocktails and cabanas... but the reality is so much more amazing!"

"Thank you, my dear," said Mr. Papadopoulos, tipping an imaginary hat in an old-fashioned but charming gesture. The resort owner was a small, dapper man, with a fondness for wearing white linen suits and gray hair pomaded like a gentleman from the 1950s. His most striking feature, however, was his magnificent moustache, which was thick and styled into two twirls on either side of his nose. Somehow, he managed to make it look distinguished rather than comical. Ellie wondered if his moustache was a nod to his Greek heritage but she didn't dare ask.

"I'm very pleased that you're enjoying my resort so much. And I'm delighted that your aunt has decided to remain here until the new year. We've never had a 'writer in residence' before," Mr. Papadopoulos said with a twinkle in his eye. "I think it gives the resort a real cachet, like having our very own Hemingway!"

Aunt Olive gave a modest laugh. "Oh, I can hardly compare to that great writer! My books are merely little mysteries—"

"They are very good mysteries," said Mr. Papadopoulos. "I have read some of them myself. It's why I was so delighted when I heard that you were staying on after the writers' conference. I'm a huge fan, Mrs. Goldberg."

"Thank you! And please, do call me Olive," said Aunt Olive, giving him a flirtatious smile.

"That's a charming vintage name which you don't often hear nowadays," said Mr. Papadopoulos gallantly. He turned to Ellie. "And yours is a nickname too, Ms. Bishop?"

Ellie nodded. "Yes, Ellie is short for Elinor, but no one has ever called me that, except my parents when I was in trouble," she added with a grin.

"In any case, you already have your own Hemingway," said Aunt Olive with a chuckle. "And he has already made your resort famous around the world!"

"Or *in*famous, perhaps," said Mr. Papadopoulos with a wry laugh. "Yes, it's not everywhere that you can eat breakfast with a scarlet macaw perched on your shoulder, demanding helpings from your plate! Although I have to say, I do worry sometimes that Hemingway might annoy the guests and put people off coming. He can be very mischievous. I know the Sunset Palms Beach Resort has built a reputation as a place for 'animal lovers' but I do often wonder if I did the right thing when I decided to let Hemingway have free run of the place. Maybe I should be confining him more—"

"Oh no—everyone I've met loves him," protested Ellie. "He's such a great character. Besides, I think people expect parrots to be a bit loud and rebellious."

"Yes, they do say living with parrots is like living with a perpetual toddler—naughty and constantly demanding attention," said Mr. Papadopoulos, sighing with a mixture of exasperation and affection. "Anyway, I'm glad that you enjoy his antics. And I'm delighted that you'll be staying with your aunt until the new year. I hope you will both have a wonderful stay at the resort. If there is anything you require— anything at all—just send me a message via the reception desk. I have left a note that you are very special guests."

"Oh, Mr. Papadopoulos, you are too kind!" twittered Aunt Olive, fluttering her eyelashes at him.

"No, no, it is only right, especially after what happened a week ago with the murder..." He grimaced "It's the least I can do to make amends for the unpleasant experience."

"But it wasn't your fault," said Aunt Olive. "Who knew that one of the writers at the conference would be murdered? If anything, I think you and your staff handled the whole thing remarkably well."

"I think it was your niece who handled things remarkably well," said Mr. Papadopoulos with an admiring look at Ellie. "She is a fantastic sleuth, I hear! Yes, yes, don't blush, young lady. There's no need to be modest. I'm good friends with the county sheriff and he told me that you practically helped them solve the case."

"Oh no, it was really just a bit of luck being in the right place at the right time," protested Ellie.

"Fiddle-faddle! Nothing was ever achieved just by being lucky," said Aunt Olive. "Mr. Papadopoulos is right. You've inherited my nostrils, Ellie, and you're quick to pick up clues."

"Erm... thanks," said Ellie uncertainly, staring at her aunt's flared nostrils and not sure it was a compliment.

"Listen to your aunt, young lady," said Mr. Papadopoulos, his eyes twinkling. "As a bestselling mystery author, I'm sure she knows what she's talking about when it comes to playing detective!"

"Well, I have no wish to play detective again," said Ellie, shaking her head with a laugh. "All I want to do now is enjoy the rest of my time in Florida and experience some of the things that Tampa Bay is famous for—"

"Ah! In that case, I have the perfect thing for you," said Mr. Papadopoulos. "Our Key Lime Pie Contest this weekend!"

Ellie looked at him with interest. "A Key Lime Pie Contest?"

Mr. Papadopoulos nodded. "It's an annual event that we host here at the resort. It's extremely popular. Not only with the locals, but many people come from other states to watch. It really helps to swell the numbers at the resort, as well as give us good publicity."

"Can anyone take part?" asked Ellie, intrigued.

"Yes, anyone can apply, but it's very competitive because we have so many entries, and can only accept a small number of contestants. Just being chosen for the shortlist is a great honor! Especially as it means that they'll be working with our head chef, Remy Marcel, one of the top pastry chefs in the country."

"And is he the one who judges the pies?" asked Aunt Olive.

"Ah no, Chef Marcel oversees the contest and helps the competitors, but we usually have a special guest judge come in to taste the pies and make the final decision on the winner. We try to invite a famous food critic or master chef or even a 'foodie' celebrity each year." Mr. Papadopoulos rubbed his hands together with glee. "This year we've managed to get Chad Coleman to agree to judge!"

Ellie looked at him blankly.

"You don't know him?" said Mr. Papadopoulos. "He's a well-known celebrity food critic and especially popular here in Florida. Coleman used to be a chef himself, actually; then he moved to TV and became the host for various shows on food and lifestyle channels. He has a big following, so it will be very beneficial PR for the resort to have him judge our contest." Mr. Papadopoulos paused, then added as an uncertain look crossed his face: "Actually, I hope getting Chad Coleman was a major coup and not my biggest mistake!"

"Whatever do you mean?" asked Aunt Olive, surprised.

Mr. Papadopoulos sighed. "Well, there's a sort of a... a feud between Coleman and Chef Marcel. They used to be business partners, you see. In fact, they used to run a restaurant together. But there was some problem and they fell out with each other. It seems that things have been strained between them ever since."

"What did Chef Marcel say when you told him about Coleman being the judge?" asked Aunt Olive.

Mr. Papadopoulos looked slightly sheepish. "I haven't actually told him. Marcel can be... well, he's almost like a stereotypical French chef, you know? Brilliant in the kitchen, but he's got a terrible temper. My goodness, I can't tell you the number of times the staff have had to call me in to calm him down about something." He sighed. "He doesn't pay much attention to things going on in the resort outside his kitchen and he never looks at the promotional material for the contests, so thankfully he's remained in the dark about Coleman's involvement. It's why I decided it would probably be easier to just surprise him on the day—present him with a "*fait accompli,*" as the French say. It will be so late in the day that he can't kick up much of a fuss then, and hopefully they won't see much of each other anyway. Chad Coleman won't be mixing with Marcel and the contestants during the day, when the baking is being done. He'll only arrive in the evening, during the judging and awards ceremony. So as long as they can remain civil with each other, there shouldn't be any unnecessary 'drama.'"

"Well, personally, I hope there will be lots of drama!" said Aunt Olive with an impish smile. "There's nothing a writer likes more than real-life conflict. It's a great chance to observe human nature and get inspiration for my next book," she said with a wink.

"I'm just interested in the pies," said Ellie, chuckling. "I'll never forget tasting that first slice of Key lime pie on the day I arrived in Florida."

"Ah, where was that?" asked Mr. Papadopoulos with interest.

"Here at the resort—at one of your restaurants: the *Hammerheads Bar and Grill* overlooking the pool," said Ellie. "Your lovely head waiter Sol introduced me to it. He told me it's the state pie of Florida."

"Yes, that's right," said Mr. Papadopoulos. "It's one of our state icons."

"Is it named after the Florida Keys?" asked Ellie.

"In a way. It's actually named after a type of lime that grows particularly well down there," Mr. Papadopoulos explained. "It's a bit similar to the regular Persian limes that you'd buy in the supermarket, except that it's yellow when ripe and is much smaller. It also has a sweeter, more aromatic flavor. It's what gives the pie its distinctive taste." He smiled. "They say the best place to eat it is down in Key West, but I think the version we've got up here in Tampa Bay is pretty damn good."

"It sounds delicious," commented Aunt Olive. "Will members of the public get to taste the pies made by the contestants?"

"No, I'm afraid there won't be enough pie to go around. But don't worry: my staff will be making our very own Key lime pies and we'll make sure that there's more than enough for everybody."

"I can't wait," said Ellie with relish. "It's a shame we won't get to taste the ones made by the contestants, though. I'd love to try different variations and see how the taste differs."

"Hey, you know what?" said Mr. Papadopoulos, snapping his fingers. "Why don't we do that?"

"Do what?" said Ellie, confused.

"We'll have a second award! Obviously, the main winner will be chosen by Chad Coleman, but I always hate to see the disappointment on the other contestants' faces, so this would be a great way to pick another winner." He smiled at Ellie. "And you can do the honors, young lady."

"Me?"

"Yes, yes, we can turn the whole thing into a PR opportunity!" said Mr. Papadopoulos, rubbing his hands together. "Having an amateur—a 'normal' person—as a judge, in addition to a professional, could be a great marketing point. Plus, since you're new to the country, you would have a fresh perspective. You're English, so your preferences might be very different from an American, and it would be interesting to see which one *you* think is the best pie. I'm sure the crowds will love it. So will you do it?" He looked at Ellie eagerly.

"Oh... erm... but I don't have any experience as a food critic or anything," protested Ellie. "I've never judged a competition before."

"You'll be wonderful!" said Mr. Papadopoulos, waving a hand. "All you have to do is taste the pies and pick your favorite. That's it! Oh, and look gorgeous and pose for a couple of photos too, but that should be easy for a lovely young lady like you," he added gallantly.

"I think it's a great idea," said Aunt Olive enthusiastically.

"Well... if you're sure," said Ellie. She laughed. "I'm not going to turn down the chance to eat more Key lime pie!"

"Great, that's settled," said Mr. Papadopoulos, getting up from the table. "Now, if you'll excuse me, I'm going to speak to my marketing manager about this new idea. Thank you for joining me for lunch. I look forward to seeing you ladies again soon!"

CHAPTER TWO

Ellie took a deep breath and stretched out her foot, dipping her toe into the water. It was cool and inviting, but still, she hesitated.

This is ridiculous! She told herself. Everyone else can learn how to do it—why can't I?

There were a series of wide steps leading into the huge resort swimming pool and Ellie went down these slowly, until the water came up to her waist. It felt cool and silky against her skin and she began to relax. She knew it was silly to be so nervous, but she had gotten so used to the feeling, from years of being scared of the water, that it was hard to change her thinking. Since arriving at the Sunset Palms, she had tried to venture into the pool every day and let go of her fears, but so far, it wasn't coming as easily as she'd hoped. She looked enviously at two little kids

1

who had jumped fearlessly into the pool and were now paddling carelessly though the water, splashing everyone around them. Look, even little children are just jumping in and they can't even swim properly, she told herself.

Feeling encouraged, Ellie began wading slowly across the pool, bobbing up and down as she moved through the water. She was careful not to go too far toward the other end, where the bottom of the pool began to slope away and the water got very deep. But she did dare to venture as far as the middle, where the water came up to her chin.

Ellie looked up. She could see seagulls wheeling overhead and hear their faint cries. The sky was a dazzling blue, with not a cloud in sight, and tall palm trees leaned lazily into view, their fronds swaying in the sea breeze coming off the beach. Ah, this is the life, she thought, smiling to herself. She could have been stuck in London, commuting to work on a crowded underground train and shivering in the cold and rain. Instead, she was here at one of Florida's most beautiful resorts, on a beach overlooking the Gulf of Mexico...

She relaxed even more, easing back into the water and feeling it wet the hair at the back of her head. Stretching her arms out, Ellie leaned back even farther, pretending to be floating on the surface of the water... Then suddenly her foot slipped from beneath her, tipping her backward, and she went under.

Ellie flailed in panic for a moment before her toes found the bottom of the pool again and she stood up, coughing and spluttering. She wiped the water from her face, then she realized that her sunglasses had fallen off their perch on top of her head and were now floating away!

"Oh no!" she cried in dismay.

She had only just bought this new pair of shades from the resort's gift shop yesterday. Her old sunglasses from England were made of cheap plastic and, when she'd seen these designer shades in the window display of the gift shop, she had been unable to resist splashing out on a new pair. They had been an expensive purchase—a real indulgence. An aviator style, with pink mirrored lenses that caught the light in a dazzling way, they seemed to represent her time here in Florida—colorful and exciting, glamorous and full of adventure. They were the most flamboyant thing Ellie had ever bought and she loved them.

I should have taken them off before I got into the pool, she berated herself. She started to go after the sunglasses, but they had drifted toward the deeper end. As she waded after them, she felt the bottom of the pool sloping steeply away and the water start to come above her chin. Ellie stopped. She was too scared to go any deeper. She stretched out her arms, but the sunglasses were floating just out of reach.

"Bugger..." she muttered to herself.

She was just looking around and wondering if she

could cope with the embarrassment of having to call one of the pool attendants to help, when she heard a raucous squawking. Ellie looked up at the sky again, and this time she saw an enormous red bird fly across the pool deck. It was Hemingway, the resort's resident scarlet macaw. He stretched out his huge wings and flapped them powerfully as he came to perch on one of the lounge chairs nearby.

"PEEKABOO!" he said, tilting his head to look at Ellie.

"Hello Hemingway," said Ellie, giving him a rueful smile. "I suppose you've come to laugh at me?"

At her words, the parrot arched his neck and let out a shrill: "HA HA HA HA HA!"

"Very funny," said Ellie sarcastically.

The parrot turned, his attention caught by the light glinting off the mirrored lenses of her shades floating on the water. He made an excited chattering sound, then suddenly, he spread his wings and took off. As Ellie watched in amazement, he swooped down toward the surface of the pool and, using his powerful claws, fished the sunglasses out of the water and rose up into the sky.

"Hey! Hemingway—come back!" shouted Ellie as the macaw flew across the pool deck and out toward the beach, still clutching her precious sunglasses.

She waded quickly back to the edge of the pool and hauled herself out. Grabbing a towel to wrap around her dripping body, Ellie raced after the parrot. She weaved between the cabanas and lounge chairs spread out on the deck and headed down a path which led from the landscaped grounds of the resort onto the beach.

Before reaching the open sand, the path passed through a small area filled with sand dunes, palm trees, and clumps of beach grasses and other seashore vegetation. Hemingway had stopped on a palm tree here and was perched now on one of the fronds. Ellie arrived at the foot of the tree and winced as she saw that the macaw had her sunglasses clutched in one claw and was nibbling them with his powerful beak.

"No! Hemingway, don't do that!" she wailed.

The parrot paused and cocked his head to look down at her.

"Come on—be a good boy. Give me back my sunglasses," coaxed Ellie.

"MY SUNGLASSES!" said the macaw, then continued what he was doing. Ellie heard something crack.

"No!" she gasped. "Oy! Stop that! You're going to break them!"

She looked frantically around and grabbed at a clump of sea oats, breaking off one of the tall spikes with seedheads. She flung this at Hemingway, but of course, it barely went high enough, fluttering harmlessly to land a few feet away.

"OY! STOP THAT!" squawked Hemingway, eyeballing her.

"Oooh!" Ellie glared at the parrot. She'd forgotten

how good he was at mimicking and how quickly he learned new words. In fact, she'd seen a couple of funny situations in the past week when Hemingway had embarrassed guests by repeating what they had said. It wasn't so funny when she was the target of his mischief now.

She looked around again, and this time she spied an abandoned beach ball nearby. She hurried to pick it up. It was slightly deflated, but she hoped that it would still be substantial enough. Ellie looked up and took aim, then tossed the beach ball at Hemingway.

Her aim was awful. The ball sailed harmlessly past. However, it was big enough to spook the macaw. Hemingway took off, screeching, into the sky. Ellie gave a cry of triumph, which quickly turned to a groan. The sunglasses had dropped from Hemingway's claws, but instead of falling to the sand below, they had gotten caught on the lowest fronds of the palm tree. They were still stuck up there, completely out of reach!

CHAPTER THREE

"Argh!" cried Ellie in frustration as she eyed the shades dangling just out of reach.

She tried to shake the trunk of the palm tree, but it was too thick and barely moved. Turning, she picked up the beach ball again and tossed it at the lower fronds, hoping to knock the sunglasses loose. Her aim was just as bad this time as the last: the ball struck the side of the trunk and bounced away, disappearing over a dune. Then she heard an exclamation come from behind the dune—a male voice crying out in surprise.

Yikes. Ellie hurried over and found herself looking into the startled eyes of a handsome young man sitting up in a hammock. He had obviously been dozing in the hammock, which was slung between two palm tree trunks, just out of sight around a large inkberry shrub. The beach ball must have sailed over and hit him on the head.

"What on earth...?" he said, rubbing his forehead.

"Oh, I'm so sorry!" cried Ellie, putting a hand up to her mouth. "Are you hurt? I didn't realize that anyone was—" She broke off suddenly as she recognized who it was. "Oh! It's you! What are you doing here? Shouldn't you be at your clinic?"

Dr. Blake Thornton grinned at her. "Even doctors get a day off sometimes. Although it would be nice if we could have a nap in peace."

Ellie blushed. "Yeah, sorry about that. I was trying to get my sunglasses out of the tree," she explained, indicating the tall palm behind them.

Blake squinted up at the hanging fronds. "How on earth did they get up there?"

Ellie rolled her eyes. "Hemingway. Don't ask."

Blake chuckled. "Did he steal them from your head? He's a bit of a magpie, you know. He can never resist any shiny, sparkly thing. I've got a pair of mirrored shades and he goes nuts every time he sees them. I don't wear them around the resort now, 'cos he's always trying to steal them off my head!"

"I'll have to remember that," said Ellie wryly.

Blake looked up, shading his eyes, then approached the palm tree. He was only wearing boardshorts and Ellie couldn't help admiring the way the sunlight played over his muscled chest and arms. Blake hauled himself up the trunk, bracing his bare feet against the rough bark and climbing easily. He didn't have to go far. Being easily over six feet, he only had to shimmy halfway up the trunk to reach the lowest fronds where the sunglasses were stuck. He plucked the shades out of the foliage and then, gripping them firmly, he leapt off the tree, landing in the soft sand underneath.

"Here you go," he said, handing the sunglasses to Ellie with a flourish.

"Thanks," said Ellie, giving him a grateful smile.

"Any time." Blake stepped back, shoving his hands into his pockets. "So how're you doing, Ellie? I've been looking out for you every time I passed the pool."

"You have?" said Ellie, feeling pleased.

"Yeah. I felt bad for cancelling our 'swimming lesson date.' It's been a crazy few days: one of the guests had a heart attack and needed to be rushed to the hospital, and then a kid broke a leg jumping off the jungle gym in the Pirate Playground. Then there was the guy who burned his tongue eating twenty habanero peppers trying to impress his girlfriend, and the couple who tried to reenact the *Romeo and Juliet* scene from their balcony—except that the guy was in his sixties and climbing up balconies is best left to lovesick but agile teenagers..." Blake shook his head. "And just when I thought I could catch my breath, a whole tour group got food-poisoning—"

"Food-poisoning!"

"Oh, not from any of the resort restaurants,"

Blake said quickly. "They'd gone out on a boat trip and sampled some oysters, which were obviously not fresh. By the time they came back that evening, they all felt sick and several were vomiting pretty badly. I had to monitor a few over the next few days, to make sure they were all hydrated and no one was deteriorating. Thankfully, only one person had to be admitted to the hospital for IV fluids."

"My God, life as a resort doctor is beginning to sound as exciting as life in the ER," Ellie teased.

Blake laughed. "Oh, I'll take this over the gunshot wounds and drug overdoses I used to have to deal with, any day! But it *was* weird how everything seemed to happen at once. It's one reason I've been catching up on some sleep today..." He looked earnestly at Ellie. "But I *am* really sorry I had to cancel our date. I was really looking forward to it."

Ellie looked up into Blake's warm brown eyes and felt her heart flip over in her chest. *Whoa... don't fall for him*, she reminded herself. She was only here on vacation. There was no future for her and Blake. She started to say something but was interrupted by the sound of a loud commotion. They both turned in surprise. The sounds seemed to be coming from the main resort building.

"What's going on?" asked Blake. He started up the path leading back toward the resort buildings, beckoning her to follow. "Come on!"

Ellie hurried after Blake and they joined the people who were leaving the pool deck and wandering toward the main resort building, to see what all the fuss was about. As they stepped through the double doors which led into the rear of the lobby, Ellie paused and hesitated as she remembered that she was only wearing a bikini and a damp towel wrapped around herself. But then curiosity overcame her self-consciousness and she pushed her way through the bodies until she got to the front of the crowd.

Flash bulbs went off and cameras clicked rapidly as a suave-looking, older man strode in through the front entrance. He paused and surveyed the gathered crowd with a smug smile, nodding and waving. He was obviously loving the attention and it looked like he was used to it too, turning and posing expertly for the many cameras pointing at him.

"Ah... looks like the celebrity guest judge for the Key Lime Pie Contest has arrived," said Blake from beside Ellie.

"That's Chad Coleman?" said Ellie.

She eyed the celebrity food critic again. She guessed that he was in his fifties, although his face had a strangely smooth, un-lined look, and his hair looked an unnatural shade of brown. He was tanned, with an almost orange hue to his skin, and he was wearing an expensive Versace silk shirt and smart black pants. There was a heavy gold chain just visible in the open neckline of his shirt and a flashy gold watch on his wrist. *A show-off who loves attention*, thought Ellie, not liking him very much based on first impressions.

"Have you met him before?" she asked Blake.

He shook his head. "No. I've seen a couple of his shows but I can't say that I'm a huge fan. The man's a bit too suave and smooth for my taste. But a lot of people seem to love him, especially the ladies." He chuckled. "I suppose some of it is aspirational. It isn't just about what he's eating, but the lifestyle. He had a show last year where he ate at some of the most expensive restaurants in the U.S. You know, truffle-infused this and 24-carat-gold-flecked that..." Blake made a face. "Not really my thing. I'm more of a burger and fries kind of guy. Still, I suppose as long as no one gets a case of food poisoning, then it's just 'different strokes for different folks.'"

Ellie turned back to look at Chad Coleman, watching as he began signing autographs for eager fans. She hoped that he wouldn't mind when he heard that she would be joining him as a "guest judge" in the contest. Somehow, she got the feeling that Coleman wasn't the kind of man who liked to share the limelight...

CHAPTER FOUR

The next day, Ellie eagerly presented herself at the reception, as advised by Mr. Papadopoulos. She wasn't officially required until the judging and awards ceremony later that evening, but when she was offered the chance to watch the contestants at work, she had jumped at it. She followed one of the resort staff out to the open lawn facing the beach where the contest was to take place.

Ellie had watched some baking shows on TV, of course, especially the famous *Great British Baking Show*, which featured contestants baking in a big marquee on the grounds of a beautiful English country estate. She saw now that Mr. Papadopoulos had obviously hoped to create a Florida version at the resort. A large beach pavilion had been set up in the middle of the lawn. It was decorated with seashells and hibiscus flowers to give it a tropical feel. Through the open sides of the pavilion, Ellie could see several workstations inside, each supplied with baking ingredients, plus a sink and an oven.

The contestants were already there, standing nervously beside their stations, and there was also a huge crowd of people surrounding the pavilion. They were members of the public and guests at the resort, as well as journalists, reporters, and TV crew. There was a buzz of excitement in the air and a hubbub of talk and laughter. Ellie felt a thrill of excitement. She had never been part of such a big event before.

She followed the staff member to the rear of the pavilion where a group of people were clustered around a large man wearing the traditional white smock and tall hat of a chef. He was gesticulating angrily and shouting in French, while those around him were trying their best to calm him down. Ellie saw Mr. Papadopoulos among them and as she got closer, she heard the resort owner saying:

"…please, Remy, I did not mean to upset you, but you must realize what a great coup this was for the resort! Chad Coleman is very popular and a celebrity in his own right—"

"The man is *un imbécile*! *Un cochon*!" snarled Chef Marcel. "I will not have him in my contest!"

"It's only for one night. Coleman will not be here during the day—I promise. And I will make sure that you don't even have to be near each other at the judging tonight."

"I refuse to be in the same room as him."

"Remy, please be reasonable," Mr. Papadopoulos pleaded. "It's too late now to find a new judge, and if we cancel, it will be disastrous for the resort's reputation! Whereas if this event gets great coverage in the media, it will be a great boost to your name and prestige too. We can use Coleman. He has a huge following and a lot of influence in culinary circles."

"*Quel faux cul!* He knows nothing about food! Nothing!"

Chef Marcel glared at everyone around him, his chest heaving. He was a big man, with an even bigger belly, and his ginger hair and moustache made him look a bit like a Viking. His big, beefy hands looked like they could easily handle a Viking hammer too. Ellie decided that she wouldn't want to get on the wrong side of him!

It seemed, though, that Mr. Papadopoulos's words had had their effect. After a few more moments of soothing persuasion, Chef Marcel grudgingly accepted Coleman's presence at the contest. Ellie stepped forward nervously as Mr. Papadopoulos then presented her as the "judge for the alternative prize." After his reaction to Coleman, she was half expecting Chef Marcel to blast her lack of experience. But to her relief, he barely gave her a cursory glance before nodding and turning away, obviously impatient to get on with the contest.

The staff and support crew performed their last-minute adjustments, the make-up artist dusted Chef

Marcel's nose with powder one last time, then there was a fanfare of trumpets announcing the start of the contest. A glamorous-looking blonde woman with a microphone walked to the front of the pavilion and stood in front of the crowds. She faced a TV camera crew, which had followed her, and as the music faded away, she gave a big smile and began to talk. Ellie guessed that she was a local news reporter, and she was obviously the host of the show that was going to broadcast the pie contest.

"This is Barbara Watts, live from the Sunset Palms Beach Resort, where the annual Key Lime Pie Contest is just about to begin! You can hear, you can see, you can *feel* the excitement in the air, as all the contestants get ready to create their version of the great Florida state icon!"

Barbara walked over to the nearest station, as she continued speaking: "And now, let's meet a few of the contestants!"

A skinny, middle-aged woman was obsessively checking her equipment and supplies at the first workstation. She barely paid any attention to the camera or Barbara Watts as she squinted at the labels on the various cans and packets of ingredients arranged across the countertop.

"Here we have our first contestant: Angela Brewer. Now, Angela, this isn't your first competition, is it?" Barbara asked with a coy smile.

"No," said Angela shortly.

"Right, I hear that you're quite the contest junkie!

You've been entering baking contests up and down the country, haven't you?"

"Yes. I'm good at baking—and I usually win," Angela said grimly.

Barbara looked a bit taken aback. "Ah, right. So you think you're going to win this time?"

"Of course. I'm the best baker here."

Barbara raised her eyebrows. "Well, I guess that remains to be seen, but we all like a bit of confidence! And I hear that you're not a Florida native, are you? You only come to stay in Tampa Bay every winter. Do you think you could take on a local dessert?"

Angela raised her chin. "Why not? I've spent way more time studying the recipe than any of the locals. I have as good a chance to win. As long as the judging is fair," she added with a dark look.

"Uh... well, I'm sure you'll be in good hands with Chad Coleman," said Barbara, hastily moving on to the next workstation. "And here we have Melanie Caruso, from Albany, Georgia. Melanie's a homemaker, the mother of two adorable little boys, and she loves to bake in her spare time. Melanie, how excited are you to be here?"

Barbara Watts pointed the microphone at a young woman who was nervously fumbling with a large padded bag—the kind of diaper bag that new mothers often lugged around. In fact, as the woman's hands slipped and she lost hold of one of the straps, the bag fell open and a packet of wet wipes, a child's plush toy, a pacifier, and a jar of baby food fell out.

"Oh! I... I'm sorry... excuse me," Melanie stammered, hastily picking the objects up and stacking them on her workstation. "Um... yes, I'm very excited... Sorry, it was such an early start this morning and I rushed out and grabbed the wrong bag. Now I've got all my kids' stuff instead of my handbag..." She blushed even more, then seemed to remember the camera trained on her and hastily straightened, pushing back her flyway blonde hair. She gave a tentative smile. "This is my first time competing in anything and I hope I might be able to win the prize."

"That's an all-expenses paid family vacation here at the Sunset Palms Beach Resort, right?" said Barbara. "I'll bet your boys would love that! How old are they?"

"Uh... they're two and four."

"And are they here today?"

A shadow crossed Melanie's face. "No, we couldn't afford to all come. But they're watching me at home on TV." She hesitated. "Can I say hi to them?"

"Sure!" Barbara gestured to the camera lens.

"Hi Jerry! Hi Matt! Mommy loves you!" said Melanie, blowing kisses at the camera.

Barbara Watts moved on to the next workstation. This was occupied by a young man with dark brown hair and a wispy beard, who was shifting his weight nervously from foot to foot.

"And this is Phil Garcia, who is actually a local from North Tampa!"

The crowd cheered.

"Nice to meet you, Phil," said Barbara, shaking his hand. "This is pretty different from what you normally do, isn't it?"

Phil seemed intensely embarrassed to be on camera. He looked down and mumbled, "Yeah... uh... I'm a biology teacher. I'm normally dissecting frogs and things in a school lab."

The crowd laughed.

"So what made you decide to join this contest?" asked Barbara.

"Oh... uh... well, I bake in my spare time. It's... uh... very relaxing. Then I saw the ad for the contest and I thought I'd try it out. If I could win a vacation here at the resort, that would be awesome."

"Who would you bring? You got a wife and kids? Girlfriend?"

Phil blushed. "No, actually, I'd bring my mom," he said. "Her sixtieth birthday is coming up. I'd never be able to afford a week at a luxury resort like this, so it would be really special."

A series of "*aww*"s came from the watching crowd. It was obvious that Phil had already become an audience favorite.

"Well, good luck!" said Barbara Watts, giving Phil a pat on the shoulder and moving on to the next workstation.

This time, there was an older man who was checking the dials on his oven.

"This is Jon Rodriguez. Now Jon has actually been

baking all his life... is that right?" Barbara turned to the man and held out the microphone to him.

"Yeah. My mama used to love baking and I remember as a little boy helping her in the kitchen. It just sort of stuck. Then my wife saw the ad for this contest and she said I should apply." He grinned at Barbara. "You know what they say: always listen to your wife."

The crowd laughed and a few women cheered.

"And I hear that you've got a secret recipe?" asked Barbara, raising her eyebrows.

Jon nodded. "It's a Key lime pie recipe that's been in my family for generations."

"Wow, sounds great! I'll bet the judges can't wait to taste it. So who will you be bringing if you win?"

"My wife," said Jon, grinning. "Even though we live here in Florida, we've never had a chance to come to the resort." He looked out beyond the pavilion at the beach in the distance. "My wife would love it here! We've got a big anniversary coming up and it would be tremendous if I could bring her here."

"Well, we wish you the best of luck!" said Barbara Watts smoothly.

She turned to the final two workstations. One had an elderly, white-haired lady who looked a bit too frail to be standing up, baking for several hours.

"Hello... it's Betty Myers, isn't it?" asked Barbara Watts, speaking slowly and bending closer to the old lady. "I hear that you're an old hand at Key lime pies."

"That's right," said Betty, nodding. "I've made

hundreds and hundreds. I've been making Key lime pie for my family ever since I got married, for my kids and grandkids. It's our favorite dessert."

"Sounds like you've had a lot of practice!" said Barbara, laughing. "So what made you decide to join the contest?"

"My grandkids signed me up."

"Aww, how sweet! I'm sure they're super proud of you. Are they watching on TV?"

"No, they're here... Look!" Betty turned and waved to a family in the crowd. They whooped and waved back, and Ellie saw that two teenagers were holding up a homemade banner which read: "*GO Nana!*"

Barbara Watts turned toward the final workstation, where a young Asian woman was examining her nail polish. She was very pretty, with long silky black hair and dark, almond-shaped eyes. She looked up as she realized that the camera was on her at last and flushed with excitement, standing up straighter and pulling her stomach in.

"And last but not least... this is Kelly Nguyen!" said Barbara Watts brightly. "Kelly, you're one of our youngest contestants today, and like Phil, baking isn't anything like your normal day job, is it?"

Kelly giggled. "No, I'm a manicurist. I work in a nail salon. But that just means I'm, like, good with my hands," she added quickly.

"Yes, and I imagine you have great attention to detail," said Barbara with a smile. "So are you excited to be here, on this beautiful day?"

"Oh yeah!" said Kelly. "So excited! Even if I don't win, just coming here and being on TV is awesome!"

Barbara Watts laughed, then turned at last to the small group of people gathered at the top of the pavilion. She approached Chef Marcel and held the microphone out toward him.

"And now, here's Chef Remy Marcel, who will be overseeing the contestants during the contest. Tell me, Chef Marcel, you must have made a lot of Key lime pie in your time?"

The head chef's chest swelled. "Not just Key lime pie. I am an expert at creating all sorts of pies and desserts. As you know, I trained as a pastry chef at the top schools in France—"

"And you used to have your own restaurant too, didn't you? With an attached bakery?"

Chef Marcel scowled. "*Oui.* But that was a long time ago."

"Ah, right," said Barbara Watts, hastily changing the subject. "So this contest... although everyone is making the same pie, they can all put their own spin on things—is that right?"

"Yes, the rule is that they must make a Key lime pie. *Alors,* they cannot produce a cream pie or a lemon meringue pie. It must be a genuine Key lime pie. But that does not mean that they cannot come up with the twists."

"The twists?"

"*Oui, oui,* for a clever cook, there are many ways to change a basic recipe."

"But a Key lime pie only has a few ingredients," said Barbara Watts. "It's famous for being one of the easiest pies to make because you need so few things. So how can there be many variations?"

Chef Marcel gave a patronizing smile. "Ah, you will be surprised. People can be very creative. Even with a few ingredients, you can have many different options for a big difference in taste. *Alors*, for example, the traditional pie base uses the graham cracker crumbs and butter, *n'est-ce pas?* But you can add things like nuts and spices to give the base a different flavor." He kissed the tips of his fingers dramatically. "*Eh bien*, there is also the famous debate about whether one should have whipped cream or *la meringue* to top the filling on the pie. Some say the traditional recipe must use meringue, others say whipped cream is much better... We will accept both versions and allow the contestants to make their own choices."

Barbara Watts turned back to the camera and spoke: "I'm sure we're all going to be waiting with bated breath to see what the contestants come up with!" She looked up at a large clock that was hanging in full view on one side of the pavilion and began to do a countdown. The crowd quickly joined in, everybody chanting:

"...Five... Four... Three... Two... One!"

Barbara turned back to the audience, raised her arms, and shouted:

"Ready... Set... It's time to pie!"

CHAPTER FIVE

There was feverish activity at every workstation as the contestants launched themselves into the pie-making: pounding, mixing, pouring, and stirring. The crowd watched and cheered, calling out contestants' names and waving homemade signs and banners. Chef Marcel began walking around the pavilion, and after a moment's hesitation, Ellie followed his example. She wandered slowly past each workstation, watching the contestants at work.

Angela was aggressively pounding graham crackers into a fine crumb to make the base, then adding melted butter and stirring the mixture to thoroughly coat the crumbs. At the next station, Ellie saw that Melanie had already moved on to the next stage and was pressing her mixture of cracker crumbs and butter into a large pie dish. A bit beyond her, Phil the biology teacher had opted to start with the filling and was busily cracking eggs and separating the yolks from the whites. At the workstation next to him, Jon was taking Key limes out of the bowl on his counter and squeezing them for juice. Farther down the pavilion, Ellie could see Betty and Kelly both busily working on their graham-cracker crusts.

As the afternoon wore on and the temperature rose, the contestants started looking flushed, sweaty, and tense as they worked on their pies. Betty found the heat too much for her and had to drop out. Kelly spilled her pie filling and burst into tears. Jon dropped his pie just as it was finished and ready to go into the oven, and had to start from scratch again. The tension was almost palpable and Ellie felt like her nerves were being stretched to the breaking point. She was glad when the gong finally sounded and the contestants were told to put down their spatulas and step away from their workstations.

"Whew!" said Barbara Watts, looking a bit frazzled herself and a lot less well-groomed than she had that morning. "Well, that signals the end of the contestants' work time. The finished pies will now be put into the chiller, ready to be taken out and sampled at the awards ceremony this evening. This will take place tonight in the resort ballroom and don't forget—there are still a few tickets available! Don't miss this fabulous evening of delicious food and entertainment. There will be a sumptuous dinner buffet, featuring many Florida specialties, and, of course, for dessert there will be Key lime pie! There will be live music and dancing too, after the awards ceremony. So make sure you're there!"

***

Ellie was excited as she dressed for dinner that night. After watching the contest and seeing the way the contestants had been interviewed, she was quite nervous about her own moment in front of the camera. So she did her make-up with extra care and then spent a long time trying to decide what to wear. She had come to Florida without packing anything to wear for more dressy occasions and she hadn't had a chance to do any proper shopping yet, so her choices were pretty limited. Aside from a series of faded shorts and T-shirts, the only other thing she had brought were a couple of sundresses. But they were cheap cotton affairs and none of them looked suitable for an evening in a ballroom—especially if she was going to have get up in front of an audience and face the cameras!

Ellie was just berating herself for the hundredth time for not packing better when her aunt strolled in, dressed in a very white silk trouser suit, with her hair perfectly-styled from a salon session earlier in the day. Aunt Olive was wearing heavy eye make-up and bright red lipstick, but she managed to carry it all off with such aplomb, the whole effect was glamorous rather than garish.

"My goodness, why aren't you dressed yet, poppet?" she asked. "We're going to be late!"

"I don't know what to wear!" Ellie wailed. "Aunt Olive, I don't have anything suitable. I didn't bring any nice dresses or anything."

"Hmm... yes, we really must take you shopping. They say that International Plaza and Bay Street has some good boutiques. But that's not going to help you tonight." Aunt Olive examined the contents of Ellie's meager wardrobe critically, then she brightened. "I know! I bought a tunic-and-slacks outfit from the cruisewear catalogue last summer. It still brand new. Never worn. It's a bit small for me but it would be perfect for you."

"Tunic and slacks?" said Ellie, making a face. "No offense, Aunt Olive, but I'm not in my sixties!"

"Nothing wrong with the sixties," said Aunt Olive tartly. "Anyway, I wasn't suggesting that you wear the whole outfit, dear. You could just wear the top. It's in a kaftan-style and long enough for you to wear as a short dress. I think it could look very chic and exotic, you know."

"A kaftan-style dress?" said Ellie, intrigued.

A few minutes later, she was trying on the top that her aunt had brought for her. As she smoothed it down and looked at herself in the mirror, Ellie was surprised to see how good she looked. The tunic top was a lovely teal green and it came down to just above her knees. The V-shaped collar had sequins along the border, which sparkled and caught the light. It was a bit baggy, but that was easily solved by cinching her waist in with a gold braid belt that her aunt had given her.

"You look fabulous, dear," gushed Aunt Olive.

"Thanks!" said Ellie. Then she groaned. "But look at my hair!"

Ever since coming to Florida, the humidity had played havoc with her already frizzy mop of curls. Now it looked like a wild halo around her head. Ellie scraped it back from her face and held it for a moment, wondering how to style it. Then she brightened as she remembered the shell-shaped clasp that she had bought from the gift shop a few days ago. Hurrying to get this from her bathroom, she clipped the mass of curls to the top of her head. Then she turned her head from side to side, pleased with the effect. The hairstyle emphasized the graceful line of her neck and shoulders, and she was delighted to see that she was beginning to develop a slight tan.

"Do you think I need a cardigan?" she asked Aunt Olive as they stepped out of their villa suite.

Aunt Olive wrinkled her nose. "A cardigan? I thought you said you're not in your sixties!" She reached out and deliberately pulled the kaftan down on one side, so that it exposed one of Ellie's shoulders. "There! You want to show off your body, poppet, not cover it all up. Besides, we're in Florida. It's so warm!" she added, gesturing to the balmy night air around them.

Ellie laughed to herself. She should have known. Most seniors would have been worried about you catching a chill and telling you to dress warmer... but not Aunt Olive! Still, when they reached the ballroom, she was dismayed to discover that her fears had been justified. The air conditioning was blasting from vents across the room and she shivered as goosebumps rose on her skin.

"I think I'd better pop back to the room and get a wrap," she said ruefully. "I'll be right back."

"All right. I'll go and nab a table at the front," said Aunt Olive, nodding toward the top of the room where a makeshift stage had been set up. There was a small podium and a long trestle table covered with a white tablecloth, where the pies were obviously going to be displayed.

Ellie hurried out of the ballroom, which was already beginning to fill with excited guests and spectators. She began making her way back across the resort grounds. She was lucky that since Aunt Olive was a rich widow, they were staying in some of the nicest accommodations. Their suite was situated in the Beach Villa Wing, on the beach side of the property. It overlooked the swimming pool and resort complex on one side and the open ocean on the other. They were close to the action if they wanted to join in, but also had privacy and seclusion away from the main resort crowds.

The only downside was that the villas were a

longer walk away from the main resort building, but Ellie didn't mind. It was a lovely evening with twilight just falling and a balmy breeze stirring through the palm trees. She hummed to herself as she strolled down the pathways, past various terraced units. As she walked past the pool, which was unusually deserted this evening, Ellie paused to admire the silhouettes of the palm trees in the distance, outlined against a pinky-purple sky. She took a deep breath and was just about to exhale in a happy sigh when she felt something rub against her bare legs. She yelped with fright and surprise, and jumped back.

"*MIAOW!*"

"Oh, it's you!" cried Ellie, clutching her chest as she looked down and saw a black cat with big green eyes looking up at her.

She gave the resort cat a mock glare. "Mojito, you've got to stop sneaking up on me like that! You're going to give me a heart attack one of these days."

She bent and patted the cat, who purred like a car engine. Ellie smiled to herself as she listened to the sound. She liked cats. Her parents had had a cat when she was growing up: a grumpy gray tabby who hogged the best spot on the couches. He had never been that friendly, but she had fond memories of stroking his soft fur (when he let her) and feeding him some of his favorite treat: smoked mackerel. She'd missed having a pet since leaving home and she had been delighted to discover that the Sunset Palms Beach Resort had a quirky reputation as the "animal lover's vacation paradise," with its resident parrot and cat, and lots of other native wildlife on the grounds.

At last, Ellie straightened and continued on her way. When she got back to the villa, it took her a while to find the cardigan that she was looking for. She thought it was in her suitcase, but after rummaging for several minutes, decided that it wasn't there. She then spent several minutes searching the whole villa, before finally finding the cardigan bundled up exactly where she'd originally first looked. She had missed it because it had been rolled up in another garment. Frustrated with herself, she grabbed it and left the villa.

As Ellie began to hurry back across the resort grounds, she glanced at her watch. She had been much longer than she'd expected and she was worried now that she might miss the start of the awards ceremony. It would be terrible if one of the guest judges was missing! She decided to take a shortcut that she knew, which detoured around the main resort buildings and wound past the rear entrance of the ballroom. It was a less scenic route, passing many of the trade and service doors, and staff parking lots at the rear of the complex, but it would be a lot quicker.

Ellie was just walking down a path which approached the rear of the ballroom when she heard a commotion. It was a woman's voice, hissing in annoyance, coupled with a familiar squawking. A minute later, she saw a woman on the path ahead of her. The woman was waving her arms angrily at Hemingway, who was flapping around her, swooping down and rising up, in a sort of game.

Ellie was just about to go up and offer to help, when the woman grabbed a bottle of perfume from her handbag and sprayed it at the parrot. Hemingway screeched in indignation, but the heavy fragrance obviously did the trick of deterring him because he turned in midair and flew off, leaving the woman standing and panting.

Ellie started toward her again, to ask if she was all right, but as the woman heard the sound of her footsteps, she whirled in alarm. She was beautiful, with high cheekbones and dark eyes set in a pale oval face. An expression of fear and dismay crossed her face as she saw Ellie and she ducked quickly sideways, disappearing into the surrounding greenery.

Ellie hurried over to where the woman had been. There was no sign of her, other than the lingering scent of the perfume she had sprayed. The area around them was deserted. Ellie peered into the dense foliage beside the path, but her eyes couldn't make out anything in the green gloom.

Who is she? Ellie wondered. The woman hadn't been in the standard khaki-and-polo-shirt "uniform" of the resort staff—she had been wearing a dark mackintosh which, even from a distance, looked expensive, and Ellie was sure that she had seen high heels on the woman's feet. *She obviously didn't want to be seen—that's why she acted so furtively and dived for cover as soon as she heard me coming. Was she one of the guests? But if so, why was she skulking here by the rear of the ballroom?*

Ellie looked thoughtfully at the path. It led past the rear service entrance of the ballroom, where resort staff could bring in carts of food or carry furniture and other equipment, or workers could come and go for maintenance and repairs. The path continued around the large oval-shaped building, coming out onto the landing at the front where wide steps led up to the main entrance. If the woman had been a guest, she should have been heading for the front entrance, not skulking around here.

Well, no time to stand here puzzling over the mystery, Ellie reminded herself. She had a pie contest to judge! Putting the strange woman from her mind, she followed the path around the ballroom and came out in front, where she quickly mounted the wide steps and hurried inside.

CHAPTER SIX

The ballroom was heaving with people when Ellie stepped inside. She weaved between tables packed with guests until she got to the one near the makeshift stage, where Aunt Olive was sitting.

"You've been ages, poppet!" said her aunt as Ellie slid into the seat next to her.

"Sorry, it took a while to find my cardigan. Did I miss anything?"

"No, the judging hasn't started yet. But you nearly missed the stone crab."

"Stone crab?"

"It's a famous Florida delicacy. I didn't fancy any tonight, but I saved you some," Aunt Olive said, pushing a plate of cooked crab claws toward Ellie.

Ellie's stomach growled. Lunch was a long time ago and she'd had a long afternoon—she was starving. Eagerly, she picked up a claw in one hand and was just wondering how to crack it when she heard a familiar voice saying over her shoulder:

"Aha! So you're sampling another of our famous local dishes, eh?"

Ellie swung around and found herself looking at a middle-aged black man. She was normally used to seeing him in the khaki-and-aquamarine polo-shirt combo worn by the wait staff at the resort's restaurant overlooking the pool, but tonight he was wearing a more traditional black-and-white waiter's uniform.

"Sol!" she said, breaking into a delighted smile. "How nice to see you! But what are you doing here? I thought you worked over by the pool?"

Sol nodded a greeting. "Yeah, that's right. But they drafted some of us over to help out here tonight." He glanced around the ballroom. "This event seems to get busier every year."

"Aunt Olive, have you met Sol? He's the head waiter at *Hammerheads Bar and Grill...* and he's my personal guide to local cuisine," Ellie added with a laugh. "He gave me some great tips on Florida's most famous dishes when I first arrived—like the Cuban sandwich and Key lime pie."

"And I hear that you're gonna be judging the pie contest tonight," said Sol.

"How did you know that?" said Ellie, surprised.

His grin widened. "Resort grapevine. Better than the top news channels."

"Never mind the pie—first you've got to taste this crab!" said Aunt Olive, gesturing to the claw in Ellie's hand.

Ellie looked up at Sol. "How do I crack it?"

"You'd normally use something like a metal lobster cracker, but here, you don't need to. We pre-crack all the claws for our guests, just to make things easier," said Sol, pointing at the joints on the claw. "The shell's left on, to protect the meat, but you just need to pull it right off... there, see?"

Ellie held up the extracted crab meat triumphantly. "Hah! I got it!"

"You got any mustard sauce?" asked Sol, looking at their table. "You can't have stone crab without mustard sauce!"

Aunt Olive made a tutting sound. "Oh, I forgot to get some of that from the buffet."

"No problem. I'll be right back," said Sol. He returned a few minutes later and placed a small bowl containing a creamy yellow-brown sauce in front of Ellie.

"What's in that?" asked Ellie, eying it without much enthusiasm.

"It's a special mix of dry mustard, Worcestershire sauce, mayonnaise, sour cream, some lemon juice, and a bit of hot sauce... oh, and a bit of salt and pepper. Go on, try it," urged Sol.

Ellie tentatively dipped a bit of the crab meat in the sauce, then popped it into her mouth. She leaned back and chewed appreciatively: the meat was sweet and tender, and the sauce had a wonderful mix of tangy and spicy flavors.

"Mm-mm... it's delicious!" she said, swallowing and taking another bite.

Sol smiled with pleasure. Then he glanced toward the stage and said: "Uh-oh... looks like you might have to finish the rest later. The judging is about to begin."

Ellie looked up and saw that Barbara Watts, the news reporter from earlier in the day, was back. She had changed into a glamorous evening gown and had her hair done, and was now twirling on stage like a movie star at the Oscars. The camera crew followed her as she went up to the group of contestants who had just joined her. They, too, had all changed into smarter clothes, and they looked nervous as they each took up a position next to the trestle table, where the finished Key lime pies stood in a row. Ellie frowned as she counted the pies. There seemed to be fewer than she'd expected. Then she remembered that Betty Myers had been obliged to drop out halfway through the afternoon. And now, as she scanned the contestants, she realized that Jon Rodriguez was missing as well. There were only four pies on the trestle table, corresponding to the four remaining contestants: Melanie, Angela, Phil, and Kelly.

Ellie hastily swallowed and wiped her mouth with a napkin, then got up from her seat and hurried to join the group of people on the stage. Mr.

Papadopoulos had decided in the end to keep his idea for a second judge and award as a secret from the contestants. He thought it would be a nice surprise for the disappointed contestants to suddenly be given a second chance at winning, after the main winner had been announced.

So although Ellie had been around the pavilion earlier, none of the contestants knew why she was involved in the event. In fact, she could see a few of them giving her curious looks as she joined everyone on stage. But people were mostly too preoccupied to pay her much attention. There was a general sense of unease and a buzz of anxious activity on stage.

"What's going on?" she asked Melanie and Kelly, who were standing next to her.

"The guest judge—Chad Coleman—he's late," Melanie explained.

Ellie glanced across the stage to where Chef Marcel was standing by the podium. He was looking at his watch and tapping his foot irritably. A resort staff member came up to him and whispered in his ear, and he looked even more annoyed. The contestants began whispering amongst themselves.

"It's typical behavior for a celebrity," said Angela sourly. "Keeping everyone waiting for him, being all arrogant and—"

"Maybe something happened to him," suggested Phil.

"Maybe he got lost," said Kelly with a giggle.

Ellie saw more resort staff hurrying back and

forth, looking worried, and more furtive discussions with Chef Marcel. Barbara Watts was trying to distract the crowd by talking to people about their favorite pies, but it was obvious that they were getting restless. Most people had finished eating now and were eager to see the event they had come for: the judging and pie awards ceremony.

Suddenly, Ellie noticed a furtive movement closer to her, and her eyes widened as she saw Angela pull out a small piping bag from her pocket. The woman paused and glanced around, making sure nobody was watching, then she leaned forward and twisted sideways, covering the view of one of the pies with her body. Quickly, she added a few extra dollops of whipped cream to the top of the pie. A second later, the piping bag was back in Angela's pocket and she had straightened again, leaning a hip nonchalantly against the trestle table. Ellie looked around, but it seemed that no one else had noticed the woman's actions. Everybody seemed to be too distracted by the mystery of Chad Coleman's absence.

Then there was a sudden commotion by the ballroom entrance. A minute later, Ellie saw Mr. Papadopoulos appear with Chad Coleman in tow. The guest judge didn't even look apologetic as he swaggered toward the stage. He was holding a large brandy glass and a half-smoked cigar, and seemed a bit unsteady on his feet.

"Disgusting!" said Angela, watching him approach the stage. "Look at him—he's drunk! He's obviously been taking his own sweet time, enjoying a drink at the bar or something, while we were all here waiting for him. The jerk!"

Ellie saw Chef Marcel's face show a similar expression of anger and disgust, but the rest of the contestants just looked pleased to finally continue the event, and the resort staff looked relieved as well that the situation had been resolved.

Barbara Watts stepped up to the podium and her voice filled the ballroom as she spoke into the microphone:

"Looks like it's finally time to get this show on the road! I know you're all as excited as I am to be here this evening. We can't wait to find out who's going to win this year's Sunset Palms Beach Resort 'Key Lime Pie Contest'!"

She paused, then assumed a sorrowful expression. "Unfortunately, two of the contestants have had to drop out: Betty found the heat a bit too much for her, and her family have taken her home to rest. And Jon was forced to start again from scratch when he dropped his pie; he never managed to complete the second one by the end of the contest. So he has decided to pull out. A real shame. But let's give a round of applause for our two unlucky contestants—making the shortlist and getting to the contest was still a great achievement!"

There was clapping and cheering from the crowd, and a couple of shouts of "Go Betty! Go Jon!" before they fell silent again.

Barbara Watts turned to Chad Coleman. "Now, here is our guest judge—the famous TV celebrity and food critic Chad Coleman!" She thrust her microphone at him. "Mr. Coleman, I'm sure you're very excited to be here and very honored to be judging this contest?"

"I think it's more a case of the resort being honored to have me as their guest judge," said Chad Coleman smugly. "I have a very busy schedule, you know. But being a Florida native, I decided to squeeze in some time to help out with this contest."

"And what will you be looking for when you judge the pies?" asked Barbara Watts.

"Well, taste is the first thing, of course. There's no point in something looking great if it tastes like crap. But presentation is important too. I mean, if something looks awful, then nobody is going to want to taste it in the first place, right?"

The crowd gave a dutiful laugh. Chef Marcel had crossed his arms and looked like he was fuming, but he didn't say anything. Barbara Watts stepped back to let Chad Coleman approach the trestle table. He swayed slightly as he walked over to the pies, and Ellie remembered what Angela had said earlier. The man did look like he had been drinking heavily; in fact, he still carried his glass of brandy in one hand as he began tasting the pies.

All the contestants watched Coleman nervously as he paused beside each pie and leaned over it, his nostrils flaring as he sniffed noisily. Then he took a fork and cut a piece out of each to taste.

"Hmm... interesting... vanilla, eh? Mmm-mm... pecan and walnuts, good texture... Ugh! Too sweet... Hmm... not bad, not bad..."

Coleman chewed slowly and thoughtfully, then went back for a second taste of each pie. Everyone watched him with bated breath. He was taking liberal swallows of his brandy glass between each bite, and to Ellie, it looked as if he got drunker and drunker with every mouthful. Finally, he staggered back to the podium and leaned heavily on it. He looked slightly sick from eating so much.

"Well... I've tasted all the entries now," he said, slurring his words. "Not bad, for a bunch of amateurs... some interesting flavor combinations..." He paused for a moment, as if gathering his thoughts, before continuing. "So... congratulations to all the contestants for their efforts. Of course, there can only be one winner..." He stopped again, and Ellie began to wonder if he was struggling to concentrate and produce a coherent sentence because he had drunk so much!

Coleman made an effort to pull himself upright. Clearing his throat, he said: "Having tasted all the pies, I can tell you that there is one which is definitely the best... And that pie is..." He paused and tugged at his collar, looking uncomfortable. "And that pie is..."

Everybody held their breath, waiting for his announcement. Ellie wondered if Coleman was dragging things out on purpose. He seemed like the kind of man who loved attention and would want to prolong a moment when everyone's eyes were riveted on him.

Coleman tugged at his collar again. "The... the winner... of the Sunset Palms Beach Resort 'Key Lime Pie Contest' is—"

Then, without warning, Chad Coleman keeled over sideways, straight onto the trestle table full of pies.

CHAPTER SEVEN

Coleman smashed into the trestle table, sending Key lime filling, pie crust, and whipped cream flying in every direction. The table broke and crashed to the floor, with Coleman's body crumpled on top of the mess of pie crusts, tablecloth, and whipped cream. There were screams and cries of horror from the crowd. Several guests sprang up and hurried toward the stage, just as hordes of resort staff rushed forward to help.

Someone shouted for an ambulance, and someone else yelled for a first-aid kit. A couple of waiters came running with glasses of water, and Ellie saw Sol attempt to lift Chad Coleman's body out of the mess. She hovered uncertainly with the other contestants, wanting to help, but not quite sure what to do. Then she heard someone shout:

"Get the resort doctor!"

Yes, of course, thought Ellie. *Get Blake! He'll know what to do.*

A few minutes later, the tall figure of Blake Thornton hurried into the ballroom. Everyone parted to let him through. He knelt down beside Chad Coleman's prone figure. The guest judge had been pulled out of the wreckage of the broken trestle table and laid at the side of the stage. Blake swiftly checked the man's pulse and other vital signs. Ellie saw that his face was grim.

"Has he had a heart attack? What happened?" asked Mr. Papadopoulos, coming forward, his face creased with worry.

"I'm not sure," said Blake. "At a guess, I would say heart attack, but it's difficult to tell without further tests."

"The ambulance will be here any minute," said Mr. Papadopoulos.

Blake didn't answer, but it was obvious from the expression on his face that the ambulance would be too late. Chad Coleman was dead. A dark mood settled on the ballroom. By the time the ambulance arrived, everyone could only watch in numb shock as paramedics transported Coleman's body out on a stretcher. Slowly, the guests packed up their things and prepared to leave. As Ellie walked out with her aunt, she caught sight of Barbara Watts standing on the front steps of the ballroom, facing the TV camera. The woman didn't seem very upset about Coleman's death or that the contest had been sabotaged. Instead, her eyes were practically glowing as she talked animatedly to the lens fixed on her.

Well, I suppose covering a dramatic sudden death is a lot more exciting than a local pie contest, thought Ellie. The news reporter was obviously making the most of her sudden scoop.

"This is Barbara Watts coming to you live from the Sunset Palms Beach Resort, where dramatic events have unfolded this evening. The resort's annual Key Lime Pie Contest has ended in sudden tragedy!" she said breathlessly to the camera. "Guest judge and celebrity food critic Chad Coleman was about to announce the winner when he collapsed on stage. By the time the ambulance arrived, it was too late to save Mr. Coleman. Witnesses say that the man appeared to have arrived at the event already under the influence and it is believed that he may have suffered a heart attack."

Barbara Watts gestured to the crowd of people streaming out of the entrance behind her. "Those who were here this evening have been in a state of shock at having witnessed the death of such a prominent local figure. Mr. Coleman is a popular TV personality as well as a celebrity food critic. Stay tuned as we bring you further updates on this tragic accident—"

"That was no accident," Aunt Olive muttered as they passed the news reporter and TV crew, and descended the steps.

"What d'you mean?" Ellie asked in surprise.

Aunt Olive tapped the side of her nose. "I can feel it in my nostrils."

"Your *nostrils*?" Ellie rolled her eyes.

Her aunt ignored her. "There was foul play involved. I wouldn't be surprised if it turns out that Chad Coleman's death was murder."

"Murder?" Ellie scoffed. "Aw, come on, Aunt Olive, this isn't one of your books! The man just had a heart attack. Anyone could see that he was drinking way too much. Isn't, like, excessive alcohol consumption a risk factor for heart disease?"

"That might be true, but heart disease isn't what killed Chad Coleman tonight."

Ellie dismissed her aunt's words and didn't think about them again as she prepared for bed. She wasn't sure if she was disappointed that she hadn't gotten the chance to judge the pies. Although it would probably have been a fun exercise, she wasn't really sorry to escape the limelight. But at breakfast the next day, Ellie found that she hadn't escaped it that easily. They had just returned to their table, with their plates heaped high from the breakfast buffet, when Mr. Papadopoulos appeared and asked to join them.

"I'm sorry about what happened last night," said Aunt Olive sympathetically. "It must be the worst kind of publicity for the resort."

Mr. Papadopoulos shook his head. "It's a terrible business, a terrible business." Then he brightened and said, "But the committee met this morning and we have agreed that we can't just let the contest end like that. For one thing, it would be very unfair to the contestants who worked so hard to enter, and many of whom have come from so far away. So we've decided that we will do a rematch this afternoon."

"A rematch?" Ellie looked at him in puzzlement. "You mean, like, do the whole contest again?"

"Yes, sort of. We'll allow the contestants the chance to bake their pies again. It won't be such a big event this time, of course, out of respect for what happened. But I'm sure Chad Coleman would have supported this decision. He was always a big believer in the saying: 'the show must go on'—in fact, we can even say that we're having a rematch in his honor."

"But you haven't got a judge anymore," Ellie pointed out.

Mr. Papadopoulos smiled. "Ah... That's where you come in, Ms. Bishop. You were going to do some judging anyway. Well, now we will simply make you the main judge."

"Me?" Ellie shook her head. "Oh, no, no, I can't be the main judge! I'm not a food critic or a chef or even an amateur baker! You must have someone better qualified than me to do the main judging."

"Yes, but none of them would have the same meaning. If I quickly got another celebrity to come and do the judging now, it would look very disrespectful. It would look completely cold-hearted, as if I had simply replaced Coleman. But you're different. You were already involved in the contest anyway, so everyone would just see it as you stepping into the breach."

"I think Mr. Papadopoulos is right," said Aunt Olive. "The contestants deserve to have their efforts judged, and the chance to win the prize that they entered for. You'd be helping to give them that chance."

"Well... I suppose, when you put it like that," said Ellie reluctantly.

So she found herself having a strange sense of déjà vu that afternoon as the entire pie-making contest was repeated in the pavilion. It was a much smaller event this time: there were no crowds or live news coverage, but Ellie still felt a weight of responsibility as she walked around the workstations and watched the contestants pounding graham crackers, squeezing Key lime juice, and mixing condensed milk and egg yolks. She was glad that this time, there would be no big awards ceremony in the ballroom. Instead, a corner of the lobby was ringed off and set up for the judging, and the only "media" present would be a few small local papers and the resort marketing manager with her phone camera.

Still, Ellie was nervous that evening as she approached the trestle table and gazed at the row of Key lime pies laid out in front of her. Some were large and some were small, some had a dark brown crust, others had a pale beige, some had a whipped cream topping and others sported meringue, and a few had slices of Key lime as garnishes on top of the pie.

Ellie had been excited originally to taste the different variations of Florida's iconic dessert, but after everything that had happened, she felt like she'd lost her appetite for the famous pie. Still, she was determined to do her duty, so she picked up a fork and approached the first of the pies. She was just scooping up the first bite and raising it to her mouth when there was a commotion outside the front entrance of the resort. People were milling about excitedly. Then the next minute, Ellie heard her name being shouted:

"Ellie! Stop! Don't eat anything!"

She froze, with the fork halfway to her mouth, and looked up in surprise to see Blake Thornton pushing his way through the crowd. He rushed over and stopped in front of her, panting heavily.

"Have you eaten any of the pies yet?" he demanded.

"No, not yet," said Ellie in surprise, lowering her fork. "I was just about to start tasting—"

"Thank God I got here in time!" said Blake.

"What d'you mean? Why shouldn't I eat the pies?"

"Because I've just come from the police station," said Blake, still panting. "They've done an autopsy on Chad Coleman and they just got the results of the tox screen. It looks like Coleman didn't die of a heart attack after all—at least, not from natural causes. There were large amounts of ethylene glycol found in his system."

"Ethylene glycol?" said Ellie, frowning.

"It's also known as antifreeze. It's extremely poisonous and, in high concentrations, it causes respiratory arrest and organ failure." Blake looked grimly at Ellie. "Chad Coleman's death wasn't an accident. He was poisoned."

CHAPTER EIGHT

"Detective Carson is ready to see you now."

Ellie got up and followed the officer down the corridor which served the inner offices of the resort. As she was being shown to a small conference room at the end of the corridor, a woman came out from the same room. She had obviously just finished being interviewed and now she brushed past Ellie without a glance.

Ellie, however, paused and did a double take. The woman looked incredibly familiar. With her pale oval face, large, dark eyes, and tall, leggy figure, she had the kind of looks that usually turned heads. Ellie wondered if the woman was a model that she'd seen in magazine features. *She even walks like a model*, Ellie thought, watching the woman sashay past her and down the corridor, swinging her hips from side to side.

A cloud of perfume wafted after her and Ellie froze as she caught the fragrance. Suddenly, she remembered exactly where she had seen the woman: on the night before last, when she was coming back to the ballroom after fetching her cardigan. This was the woman who had been having a tussle with Hemingway on the path by the rear of the ballroom. She had pulled out a bottle of perfume from her handbag and sprayed it at the parrot to scare him away—and Ellie had caught some of the lingering scent. She recognized the same fragrance now.

As soon as Ellie entered the conference room, she couldn't help blurting out: "The woman who just left—who is she?"

Detective Carson looked surprised. "That's Talisha Coleman, Chad Coleman's wife. Why do you ask?"

"I'm sure I saw her last night, here at the resort," said Ellie. "She was outside the rear doors of the ballroom."

"That's impossible. Mrs. Coleman was home all night last night."

"Are you sure?"

Carson looked annoyed. "Of course I'm sure. I just questioned her."

"Yes, but how do you know she's telling the truth?"

"Ms. Bishop…" Carson gave her a patronizing look. "I realize you're not from the States so you might not know how investigators work here. Let me tell you, I've worked enough homicide cases to know when a woman is lying."

Maybe not when the woman is as beautiful as Talisha Coleman, thought Ellie cynically. Still, she could see that there was no point in continuing to press him on the subject. Instead, she said: "You wanted to see me?"

"Yes. I know I questioned you briefly before, but I'd like to ask you some more questions about the Key Lime Pie Contest and the night of Chad Coleman's murder."

For the next half-hour, Ellie went over the events of the past two days, from when she had arrived at the pavilion for the first round of the contest, to yesterday evening when she had been about to start tasting the pies after the second round.

"It's lucky Dr. Thornton stopped you before you tasted anything," said Detective Carson. "You could have been poisoned too. As it turned out, we tested the second batch of pies and they were all fine. But one of them was definitely poisoned when Coleman was tasting them."

"Are you sure the poison was in one of the pies?" asked Ellie. "Couldn't it have been in the brandy Coleman was drinking?"

"No, the autopsy found pieces of Key lime pie in his stomach which contained high levels of antifreeze. Someone had deliberately laced one of the pies with ethylene glycol. But we don't know which pie those pieces are from, which means we don't know who poisoned him."

"Can't you test the original pies to compare?"

"They're all in the garbage!" said Carson in frustration. "Coleman fell onto the trestle table holding the pies. Everything crashed to the floor and was smashed together. When the resort staff cleaned everything up, they just scooped up the mess and dumped it in the trash. So all the different pies got mixed together."

"But didn't you keep the pies to analyze?" asked Ellie. "I thought that's what forensic teams do."

Carson glowered at her. "They do when they suspect foul play. They contain the crime scene and preserve samples for analysis. But in this case, nobody thought Coleman's death was suspicious at first. It looked just like a heart attack! It wasn't until the next day when we discovered high levels of ethylene glycol in his system that we suspected poisoning. By then, it was too late—all the mess from the ballroom had been cleaned up and thrown out in one of the resort dumpsters. Sure, we can dig up samples from the dumpster to analyze, but even if we do find some pieces with poison in them, there's no way to tell whose pie those samples came from."

He leaned forward suddenly and said: "Are you sure you didn't see Chef Marcel near any of the pies after they came on stage?"

"Yes, I'm sure. He was standing by the podium; he wasn't anywhere near the trestle table, where all the pies were placed. I told you, the only person I saw go near the pies was one of the contestants—that woman called Angela. I saw her take a piping bag out of her pocket and add something to the top of one of the pies. She acted really furtive; it was obvious she was trying to do it secretly and not let anyone see."

"I've questioned Angela Brewer," said Carson, waving a hand carelessly. "She says she was just adding some whipped cream to the top of her pie. She says it got damaged during the transport to the ballroom and she was fixing it up, because she wanted it to look perfect."

"Well, of course she would say it's only whipped cream!" said Ellie impatiently. "She's hardly going to admit to adding poison, is she?"

Carson ignored her words. Instead, he said: "You're absolutely sure that Chef Marcel couldn't have had access to any of the pies?"

Ellie looked at him in exasperation. The man was like a dog worrying a bone! "Why are you so obsessed with Chef Marcel anyway?" she asked. "Why do you think he's responsible for Coleman's murder?"

"Because there's a history of bad blood between him and the victim. They used to run a restaurant together. But Coleman made some bad decisions, borrowed a lot of money, and got the business badly into debt. And instead of doing something about it, he went behind Chef Marcel's back and got himself a lucrative TV deal. As soon as the contract was signed, he pulled out of the business, leaving Marcel with a struggling restaurant and a mother lode of debt. The recession hit, things went from bad to worse, and Marcel ended up filing for bankruptcy less than a year later."

"But surely people fail in business all the time? They don't all murder their business partners," argued Ellie.

"They might if they lost their life savings, and felt as betrayed as Marcel did. You weren't around at the time; you didn't hear what he had to say in press releases and interviews. Man, he was bitter! Ask anyone who knew about the story, if you don't believe me."

"Well, OK, even if Chef Marcel might have had reason to want Coleman dead, wouldn't it have been stupid to murder him at a contest that he—Marcel— was hosting?" asked Ellie. "I mean, that's like shining a big spotlight on yourself!"

"Actually, I think it's real clever," said Carson. "At a contest like this, he's got a lot of other people around to push the blame onto, lots of other potential suspects. Especially if he uses one of the contestant's pies to deliver the poison—it's like having a ready-made scapegoat."

"It's still seems ridiculously risky," Ellie protested. "There must be a million other ways for Chef Marcel to poison his old business partner, without having to do it on stage, in front of a live audience and TV cameras and everything. It seems crazy—"

"I don't expect a young woman like you to

understand," said Carson, giving her a condescending smile. "Now, you just keep your mind on cooking and baking, and leave the police work to real professionals, OK?"

Ellie bristled at his patronizing words, but she knew that she couldn't really argue. It was true that she wasn't a professional detective in any way. Still, as she got up and left the conference room, she couldn't help feeling that Detective Carson's smug and superior attitude would lead him to mess up in this investigation.

CHAPTER NINE

As Ellie was escorted out of the resort's inner offices, she was approached by one of the staff members who normally worked behind the reception counter.

"Ms. Bishop? Do you have a moment free? Mr. Papadopoulos would like to see you," the woman said in a low voice.

"Oh... of course," said Ellie, slightly surprised by the woman's manner.

"He's waiting for you in the courtyard just outside the rear lobby doors."

Ellie made her way outside and found the resort owner pretending to read a poster listing "Today's Activities." His face lit up when he saw her and he came quickly over.

"Thank you for coming, my dear. Sorry for all the

'cloak and dagger,' but I didn't want anyone to see me speaking to you. In fact..." He glanced around, then took her arm gently. "Shall we go for a walk down by the beach? Fewer listening ears that way."

"Oh... of course," said Ellie, filled with curiosity now.

"Have you been to our Snack Shack yet? It's out on the beach, among the sand dunes."

"No, I didn't even realize there was another eatery out there. It sounds intriguing."

"Ah, in that case, we must go!" said Mr. Papadopoulos enthusiastically. "You must taste some of our iconic snacks."

"I've only just had breakfast an hour ago," said Ellie, laughing. "And it was a big breakfast too! American breakfast buffets are incredible. If I keep eating like this, I'm going to be charged excess weight on my return flight to England!"

"Oh, a little snack never harmed anyone," said Mr. Papadopoulos, chuckling. "And the walk there and back will help to work off the calories."

Ellie soon realized that he was right. It was a fair walk to the Snack Shack, which was in an area of the resort property that had been purposefully left in its natural beach state. There were tussocks of sea oats and other beach grasses, as well as inkberry shrubs, railroad vines, and other native Florida seashore plants—all growing amongst rolling sand dunes. It was hard work plowing through the sand and, after a few steps, Ellie slipped off her sandals and continued barefoot. By the time she arrived at their destination, she was puffing from the effort. Mr. Papadopoulos, though, hardly seemed to break a sweat, despite being smartly dressed in his usual white linen suit. Ellie was slightly ashamed to discover that an elderly man was fitter than her!

It's all that sitting around in offices back in London, she thought. *Now that I'm here in Florida, I really need to get out in the fresh air and exercise more.*

The Snack Shack was a small wooden structure which had been made to look like an abandoned beachcomber shack. It was surrounded by leaning palm trees, between which were strung comfy hammocks. There were also several old wooden crates and oil barrels, as well as large pieces of driftwood and other items strategically placed around the shack to provide seats and tables, while still keeping the look and vibe of a natural beach area.

The shack itself seemed to be mostly made up of the kitchen—there was no seating room inside. Instead, there was just a window where you could put your order in and then pick up the food. Ellie saw several people lined up, waiting to receive their paper baskets of hot, crispy food, before heading to the crates and hammocks to enjoy their snacks.

"This is brilliant!" said Ellie. "What a fantastic setting!" She turned to look at the beach, which stretched in front of the shack. "This must be a great place to come and watch the sunset."

"Yes," Mr. Papadopoulos agreed. He pointed to several fire pits in the ground between the crates. "It's one of the most popular resort activities, to come here, roast some marshmallows to make s'mores, and watch the sun go down."

"Make what?"

Mr. Papadopoulos raised his eyebrows. "You've never had s'mores? You've been missing out, young lady!"

"What are they?"

Mr. Papadopoulos smacked his lips. "The most delicious thing you could ever eat," he said with a grin. "It's basically a sandwich with roasted marshmallows and chocolate between graham crackers. It's a campfire tradition in America. You can make them at home, but everyone agrees that they're much better roasted over an open fire."

"Wow, sounds like a special experience," said Ellie.

"The resort does s'mores several nights a week, providing the weather is good, so you must come out here on one of those nights and taste some. Now..." He indicated a large blackboard leaning against the shack, where someone had roughly chalked out several menu items. "What can I get you? The Snack Shack, as its name suggests, serves some classic snacks from around the country: chicken strips, potato skins, nachos, buffalo wings, and even fried clams, New England style."

"I've always loved buffalo wings, but I suppose I

should really try something that's famous in Florida?"

Mr. Papadopoulos smiled. "Ah… in that case, have you tried gator bites?"

Ellie looked at him incredulously. "You don't mean 'alligator,' do you?"

He laughed. "That's exactly what I mean. Little chunks of alligator meat, covered in batter and deep-fried."

Ellie made a face. "Erm… I'm not sure I really want to eat alligator."

"Oh, you might be surprised. They're considered a local delicacy, you know."

"What does alligator taste like?" asked Ellie.

"Different people say different things. Some people say it tastes like chicken, others say it's a bit fishy, but with a firm texture. You should really taste it for yourself. Come on," he said, looking at her persuasively. "You can't come to Florida and not try gator bites at least once."

"Oh, all right," said Ellie with a laugh. "I'm game. I'll try some gator bites."

Mr. Papadopoulos smiled, pleased. "Good! Now, we do gator bites in three different ways: blackened, which is Cajun-style, buffalo or—my personal favorite—dipped in golden breadcrumbs and deep-fried until hot and crispy."

"That last one sounds delicious! I'll go with that," said Ellie.

Ten minutes later, a basket filled with crispy

brown nuggets was placed in front of Ellie, together with a small bowl of spicy ranch sauce. She picked up one of the gator bites and popped it into her mouth, chewing slowly. She looked up to see Mr. Papadopoulos waiting expectantly.

"They're actually quite good," said Ellie in surprise. "They do taste a bit like chicken, but there's also a mild fishy flavor. They're very chewy, reminds me a bit of calamari..."

Mr. Papadopoulos watched her enjoy the gator bites for a few moments, then his face turned serious and he said: "I actually want to speak to you about the murder, my dear."

Ellie paused in her eating and looked up. "Yes?"

"I heard that the police questioned you again this morning. They seem to think my head chef Remy Marcel is responsible, right?"

Ellie nodded. "Yes, that's the impression I got. Detective Carson kept asking me over and over again if I saw Chef Marcel tampering with the pies while I was onstage. The thing is, I suppose it's logical for the police to suspect Marcel because of the... erm... history between him and Chad Coleman."

"But that was so long ago!" Mr. Papadopoulos burst out. "That fallout over their restaurant was over ten years ago. If Marcel wanted to get revenge, wouldn't he have done it when things first happened? Surely that would have been when he was most angry? Why would he have waited ten years to kill his partner?"

Ellie shrugged. "I don't know... I suppose people could say that he was stewing all this time. You know, brooding on it, and nursing his grudge, and then when he saw Chad Coleman again, it all just exploded."

"Do you believe that?" demanded Mr. Papadopoulos.

"No," Ellie admitted. "I mean, even if Chef Marcel *had* wanted to kill Coleman, I just don't get why he would have done it at his own baking contest. It seems so stupid and risky, when there are so many other ways to do it."

"Did you tell Detective Carson that?"

"Yes, but he thinks that it could have been a clever strategy on Marcel's part, because it was a way to have loads of other suspects confusing things. You know, one of the contestants would make a perfect scapegoat."

"Well, I think he's wrong!" said Mr. Papadopoulos. "I know Marcel. Aside from being an employee, he's a personal friend of mine, and I *know* he wouldn't murder anyone! Yes, I know he's got a temper—what successful chef doesn't, eh? They're known for being a volatile bunch! But that doesn't mean that he would stoop to murder."

"Maybe, once the police investigate things more, they'll agree with you."

Mr. Papadopoulos gave her a dark look. "I wouldn't count on it. They just want a quick arrest and I'm worried that while they're busy wasting time investigating Chef Marcel, the real culprit will get away. Besides, having a key member of the staff arrested on a charge of murder—even if he is found innocent later—would be terrible for the resort! As they say: 'mud sticks.' It will be a PR disaster. So..." He leaned forward and looked at Ellie earnestly. "I was wondering if I could count on your help, my dear."

"*My* help?" Ellie looked at him in puzzlement. "Help with what?"

"With finding the real killer."

Ellie gaped at him. "Pardon?"

"Listen, the police have asked all the contestants to stay in the area while the investigation is still ongoing. Since we don't know which Key lime pie the poison was in, they're all potential murder suspects at this point. So I've offered to put them up at the resort, free of charge—keeps them all in one place and makes it easier for the police to question them, keep an eye on them, etcetera." Mr. Papadopoulos made a rolling motion with his hand. "Since you're staying at the resort already, you'll probably run into the contestants just going out and about. All I'm asking you to do is keep your eyes peeled and your ears alert for anything which might help to solve the case. Maybe even talk to a few of them and see if they might blurt out anything suspicious."

"I'm not the police, though," Ellie pointed out. "I don't have the right to question people—"

"That's the whole point! I don't want you to

'question people.' Everyone clams up when the police question them. But it's different when people are just chatting with each other. I'd do it myself but, of course, it would look odd if I suddenly started going up to them and trying to act friendly. It's different for you, though—you're just one of the other guests."

"And what if I hear something suspicious about Chef Marcel?" asked Ellie.

"I'm sure you won't," said Mr. Papadopoulos. "But if you do, then of course, you must report it to the police."

Ellie hesitated, then said, "OK. I'll try my best."

Mr. Papadopoulos beamed. "Great! I knew I could count on you, Ellie." He glanced down at his watch. "Now, I'm afraid you'll have to excuse me—I have a meeting to get to. But stay as long as you want and enjoy anything else you'd like from the menu. I've already instructed the Shack staff—it's all on the house!"

CHAPTER TEN

After Mr. Papadopoulos left, Ellie sat for a few minutes by herself, thoughtfully eating the rest of her gator bites. She was almost finished when there was a rush of wind and a flurry of feathers, and the next moment, an enormous scarlet macaw landed on the crate that Mr. Papadopoulos had been sitting on.

"PEEKABOO!" said Hemingway.

"Hello Hemingway," said Ellie in delight.

Although she knew that the parrot was tame, it still felt like an honor whenever he chose to come and sit with her—like a wild animal allowing you to get close. Now she watched as the parrot waddled toward her and arched his neck, exposing the back of his head to her. Ellie smiled and obliged, reaching out to tickle his favorite spot. Hemingway closed his eyes in bliss for a few minutes, then he sat up again and ruffled his feathers.

"WHATCHA DOIN'?" he croaked.

Ellie chuckled She knew that the macaw was just repeating phrases he had learned from the guests. Still, he had an uncanny ability to say the right thing at the right time, which made it seem as if he was really talking to you.

"Nothing much. What are *you* doing?" she answered, grinning.

The parrot bobbed up and down, as if in time to imaginary music. "DANCIN'!" he croaked. He swayed from side to side, then bobbed energetically again. "DANCIN'!"

Ellie laughed out loud.

Hemingway shuffled closer and eyed Ellie intently. At first, she thought that he was interested in the last morsel of gator bite she was holding, but then she realized that the parrot was gazing avidly at her new sunglasses. She had shoved them up into her hair while talking to Mr. Papadopoulos and now they were perched precariously on her mop of curls.

"Oh no you don't—not again!" said Ellie, hastily snatching the sunglasses off her head and putting them in her pocket. She gave Hemingway a defiant grin. "There. Now you're not going to get them, unless you've got a neck like a flamingo."

"FLAMINGO!" yelled Hemingway.

"That's right, a flamingo," said Ellie.

"FREAKIN' FLAMINGOS!" screeched Hemingway. "USE YOUR IMAGINATION!"

"Huh?" Ellie looked at the macaw in confusion. "What?"

"USE YOUR IMAGINATION!" repeated the parrot. He gave another ear-piercing screech. "MOON JUICE, ARE YOU CRAZY? FREAKIN' FLAMINGOS!"

"*Shush!*" Ellie admonished, glancing around and seeing several other guests looking her way. Embarrassed, she tried to distract the parrot.

"Look, Hemingway..." She picked up her empty paper basket and shook it, making the few bits of breadcrumbs left in the bottom rattle.

The macaw perked up and shuffled closer, peering into the basket. "WANNA NUT?" he said hopefully.

"No, no nuts, although there are some breadcrumbs left," said Ellie. She picked up a small piece of the crispy breadcrumb coating and offered it to the parrot. He took it delicately in his powerful beak and nibbled at it. It crumbled quickly into fragments in the sand below. Hemingway looked disgruntled.

"WANNA NUT? WANNA NUT?" he screeched.

"All right, all right," said Ellie, hurriedly getting up and going over to the window of the Snack Shack.

She was pleased to see that they sold the resort's own special mix of nuts, flavored with hot spices. She had learned that this was Hemingway's favorite treat and she always laughed when she saw his pupils dilating from the hot taste as he ate the nuts.

"Here you go," she said, coming back with the small bowl and offering it to the parrot. "Just a few, though—I don't think it's healthy for you to have too many."

The macaw made happy chattering noises as he fished a large Brazil nut out of the mix and began expertly cracking it with his beak. Ellie watched him with a fond smile. She had to admit that although Hemingway could be loud and demanding and often behaved like a bratty child, he could also be very sweet, endearing, and entertaining. It was probably why the guests and the resort staff loved him so much and let him get away with murder.

Murder... Ellie was suddenly reminded of the mystery surrounding Chad Coleman's death. She thought of what Mr. Papadopoulos had asked her to do. *Well, there's no time like the present*, she thought, getting up from the crate.

"WHATCHA DOIN'?" said Hemingway again, stretching his wings out as he looked at her.

Ellie smiled at the parrot. "I'm going sleuthing!"

As she started walking back toward the main resort complex, her cellphone rang. Ellie's heart sank as she looked at the screen and saw her sister's name on the caller ID. Somehow, she didn't think that Karen was calling to say: "*Wish I was there!*"

She was right. She had barely answered the call when her older sister launched into a tirade:

"I couldn't believe it when I called Mum last week and she told me that you'd gone off to Florida! *Florida!* What on earth were you thinking?" Karen Bishop demanded.

"I was thinking of sunshine and lovely white sand beaches," Ellie said defensively. "I wanted to get away from the horrid winter weather in London—what's wrong with that?"

Karen made a sound of disbelief. "*What's wrong with that?* I can't believe you'd even ask that! It's just typical of you, Ellie. Always being reckless and not thinking about your responsibilities—"

"I don't have any responsibilities," said Ellie. "It's not like I'm married or have kids, like you. I don't even have a boyfriend anymore. So why shouldn't I go away if I fancy?"

"And what about your job? What about your responsibility to yourself?" demanded her sister. "It's bad enough that you've been messing around with temp jobs all year, but you can't keep doing that forever. You don't have any potential career; you don't have any stability in your future."

"I don't have a mortgage either, or children I have to pick up from school, or a husband I have to cook dinner for," retorted Ellie.

"Geoff never expects me to cook dinner for him," said Karen loftily. "I just enjoy doing it because it helps me unwind after a long day at the office."

"Yes, well, we're not all the perfect wife-mother-senior-lawyer-superwoman combo that you are," muttered Ellie.

"I never said I was a superwoman," said Karen irritably. "I just like to have things balanced in my life."

You can say that again, thought Ellie, rolling her eyes. Karen had turned achieving the perfect life balance into an Olympic sport! Out loud, she sighed and said, "You sound just like Dad. And even he agreed in the end that coming to Florida was a good idea. It's not like I booked myself on an extravagant holiday! Aunt Olive invited me to come and stay with her. She's got a two-room suite and her package at the resort is all-inclusive, so all my meals and accommodations are paid for. I would have been mad not to take up such a good offer."

"That's not a reason to do things! You have to consider everything—you have to look at the long term, not just whatever you feel like doing now, for instant gratification. Sometimes you have to refuse what looks like a good offer in order to do the sensible thing, the right thing, and—"

"You're just jealous that Aunt Olive didn't invite you," said Ellie.

"Me? Jealous? Don't be ridiculous," snapped Karen. "And I wouldn't have gone even if she *had* invited me. I've got more sense than that—"

"Well, I'm here now, whether you like it or not," cut in Ellie. "And I'm going to enjoy myself. Like I told Dad, it's only for a few weeks. I'll be coming back to the U.K. in the new year. Another few weeks is hardly going to make a difference to my 'great career future,'" she said sarcastically. "A lot of companies close down over the Christmas period anyway. Everything starts up again in January and I'll be back home then."

"I suppose so..." said Karen grudgingly. "I can't believe you decided to leave Mum and Dad alone over Christmas, though! Didn't you think that was a bit selfish?"

"They're hardly alone," protested Ellie. "They've got you and Geoff and the kids. And besides, they told me that they were thinking of going on a cruise this year. It leaves on Boxing Day. So they would have left *me* alone the day after Christmas anyway."

"You would have still had *us*," said Karen, sounding aggrieved. "Don't you want to spend some time with your niece and nephew? And I hardly see you, Ellie, the rest of the year. I was looking forward to spending more time with my little sister."

More like looking forward to spending more time lecturing me, thought Ellie sourly. Then she tried to be more charitable. She knew that in spite of her patronizing manner, Karen probably meant well. Her elder sister just couldn't understand any attitude to life that was different to her own.

"Look, it's just for this year, OK?" Ellie said, trying to sound conciliatory. "I will miss spending Christmas with you and Geoff and the kids, but this is a once-in-a-lifetime opportunity! Come on, Karen—I know it might not be the kind of thing you're into, but can't you put yourself in my shoes for once? I'm only twenty-six. I've got loads of time still to 'sort out my life.' I want the chance for a bit of adventure, while I still can."

"Well... I suppose you're right," said Karen, her tone softening slightly. There was a pause, then she said briskly: "Make sure you apply sunscreen religiously—the sun can be really strong in Florida, even in wintertime, and you know you freckle horribly. And drink lots of water! It's so easy to get dehydrated on the beach. Oh, and be careful if you go on any boat trips. Make sure you check the company's credentials: see that they have insurance, read their reviews... and they should have an emergency plan too, and show you what provisions they've made for safety equipment, like life jackets and such."

Ellie rolled her eyes. Her sister just couldn't resist getting a few bossy instructions in, even when she capitulated!

"Yes, miss," she said cheekily. "What about if I meet any alligators? Should I ask them if they've had regular dental checkups so I know their teeth are in good shape when they bite me?"

CHAPTER ELEVEN

Ellie spent the rest of the day hanging around the resort, trying to find excuses to chat with other guests and resort staff about the murder. She even spent an hour pretending to admire the fish in the big aquarium tank in the lobby, just so she could linger in the area and eavesdrop on conversations. By the time evening rolled around, she was tired and drained, but she still hadn't picked up any interesting leads.

Although she had chatted with several other guests and listened to all sorts of speculation about Chad Coleman's murder, everyone seemed to just be repeating gossip they had overheard. As for the contestants themselves, she'd seen them a few times, but they were all doing innocuous things, like lounging beside the pool. And although Mr.

Papadopoulos had encouraged her to snoop and question, Ellie hadn't felt comfortable about going up to any of the contestants and grilling them without a good excuse.

It wasn't until sunset that Ellie saw her chance. It was Happy Hour at the Tiki Bar beside the pool and Ellie was pleased to see two familiar faces among the guests eagerly waiting for cocktails. They were Melanie Caruso, the housewife from Georgia, and Kelly Nguyen, the pretty Asian girl who worked in a nail salon. They seemed to have become good friends. Ellie had seen them earlier in the day, lying together at a cabana by the pool, and now they were standing next to each other, giggling and whispering like two schoolgirls.

Ellie sidled up beside them and when they next laughed at something, she joined in, laughing loudly with them. It was a trick that she had picked up back in London—it was a great way to join conversations with random strangers at parties. As expected, Melanie and Kelly turned to look at her and smiled, thinking that she was sharing their recent joke.

"Hey, you're from the Key Lime Pie Contest, aren't you?" said Melanie.

"Yeah! You're that girl who was going to be the second judge!" Kelly cried.

"Yes." Ellie gave a slightly embarrassed smile. "Although I'm not a famous food critic or anything like Chad Coleman was. I'm just a guest here at the resort. I'm from England so the resort management thought it would be cool to have me give out a second prize—you know, like the 'foreigner's choice' of the best pie."

"Oh! I thought your accent sounded British," said Melanie.

"So when Coleman kicked the bucket, they got you to do the real thing?" asked Kelly.

Ellie nodded. "And for what it's worth, all your pies looked delicious. I'm sorry I didn't get the chance to taste any."

"Aww, that's so sweet of you," said Melanie, beaming at Ellie.

"Yeah, I'm glad you are not, like, running away from us because you think we might be murderers or something," said Kelly, making a face. "People have been acting weird around us all day. What do they think we're gonna do? Poison the cocktails?"

"Shh!" said Melanie, giggling, as several other guests at the bar counter shifted uncomfortably and gave the girls side-eye.

"Anyway, I wouldn't be surprised if the murderer turned out to be Angela," added Kelly in a hushed voice. "That woman's a total weirdo."

"What d'you mean?" asked Ellie quickly.

"She's, like, totally obsessed with winning," explained Kelly. "When we arrived at the pavilion on the day of the contest, Angela was already there. She got there, like, two hours early, just so she could check her ingredients and get used to the workspace and stuff." She rolled her eyes.

"Yes, she was going around checking the size of everyone's eggs," added Melanie. "She made Phil exchange his eggs with hers, 'cos she said his were bigger and that gave him an unfair advantage."

"She even told me that having a mascot was an unfair advantage!" said Kelly, scowling.

"A mascot?" said Ellie, confused.

Melanie giggled. "Kelly's obsessed with plushies. She's got hundreds and hundreds of them, and she even brought one along to the contest as a sort of good-luck charm. She had it on her workstation with her."

"Hey, you're making me sound like some kind of weirdo," Kelly protested. "Lots of people collect plushies. It's no big deal. Besides, you were pretty frantic yourself when you couldn't find your soft toy yesterday."

Melanie flushed. "Yes, but that was for my son. I brought it by mistake when I brought the diaper bag. He'll be really upset if I lose it."

"Well, you can give him one of my plushies if you want," said Kelly, grinning. "Not my lucky mascot, but I brought a couple of others in my case."

"There, you see?" said Melanie with a teasing look at Ellie. "Who brings stuffed toys from home when you're an adult?"

"Lots of people get comfort from plushies," said Kelly indignantly. "You know, they did research and they found, like, nearly forty percent of adults still sleep with a stuffed toy every night. Plushies aren't just toys—they've got, like, big emotional support and health benefits."

"Well, I have to admit, I have a stuffed teddy bear from childhood that I hang on to," said Ellie with a laugh. "I don't sleep with it, though!"

"Well, I like taking plushies with me everywhere and I'm not ashamed of it," said Kelly with a defiant shrug. She reached into her shoulder bag and pulled out two little plush toys in the shape of a clam and a starfish, each with a smiling face on it. "Check these out. Aren't they cute? Just looking at them cheers me up."

"Did Angela really object?" said Ellie. "I mean, that seems ludicrous... how does having a soft toy give you an unfair advantage?"

"She's a total nutcase when it comes to competitions," Kelly said, rolling her eyes. "I was talking to one of the resort staff, this dude called Sol who works at the *Hammerheads Bar and Grill*—"

"Oh yes, I know Sol!" said Ellie. "He's really lovely."

"Right. He's a cool guy. Anyway, he told me that Angela comes every year and takes part in this contest, and she always has to win. If she doesn't win, she throws a huge hissy fit."

"But surely she can't win *every* year," said Ellie.

"Oh, you'd be surprised. Sol told me, like, half the time, the guest judge gets so intimidated by Angela that he ends up awarding her the prize, just to have an easy life. 'Course, she wasn't gonna get that this year with Chad Coleman."

"What d'you mean?" asked Ellie.

"Oh, he wouldn't put up with that kind of crap! I read this article about him where he was judging another contest down in Key West. After giving out the prize, he found out that the winner had added, like, some extra stuff to her cake at the last minute—you know, after they'd been told to stop working on it. So he stripped her of her prize and banned her from the contest. She kicked up a real stink but Coleman wouldn't back down."

"That wasn't Angela, by any chance?" asked Ellie, half-jokingly.

"Nah, she was some woman from South Florida," said Kelly. "But that *could* have been Angela. Maybe she killed Coleman so he wouldn't kick her out of the contest," she said, grinning. "Anyway, it's a real bummer that they've cancelled the whole thing."

"Yes, your boys must be really disappointed," Ellie said to Melanie.

"Huh? Oh... yeah, totally," said Melanie. "They kept saying: 'Mommy's gonna win!'"

"And your hubby!" said Kelly. "He must, like, really need a vacation."

"What does he do?" asked Ellie.

"Oh, he works at a local diner," said Melanie.

"Yeah, but you told me he used to be a chef, right?" said Kelly. "You said he used to own a restaurant himself, but now he's flipping burgers at this place and the boss is a real jerk. They make him work crazy hours with, like, no overtime."

Melanie looked embarrassed. "Well, it's good he's got a job," she said quickly. "It brings in an income and that's all that matters. Didn't you say the same thing, Kelly, about your job? You said it's just a way for you to save money, so you can get out of your hometown and go traveling."

"Oh yeah!" said Kelly, tossing back her silky black hair. "Yeah, I can't wait to get out of that place."

"I felt just like you," said Ellie, pleased to find a kindred spirit. "I couldn't wait to get away from London—"

"London?" said Kelly incredulously. "Jeez, if I lived in London, I wouldn't be wanting to leave! People, like, travel from all over the world to visit London!"

Ellie laughed. "I suppose it all depends on your point of view. If you grew up in London, you might not find it so exotic and exciting. And I don't live in central London, you know, where all the famous sights are. Most of us 'regular people' live and work in the outer suburbs, which are pretty boring."

"I guess," said Kelly, still not looking convinced. "I'll bet it's still better than Springfield, Virginia, though."

"I don't know... Virginia sounds really exotic to me!" laughed Ellie.

"Hey, you know what I heard?" said Melanie brightly. "To make up for cancelling the contest this year, the resort is offering all of us contestants a confirmed place at next year's contest. Without having to go through the preliminary rounds, I mean.

So I guess we'll get another chance at winning the luxury vacation."

"Well, I'm not going through all this again," said Kelly in disgust. "I only did it 'cos I thought it would be fun, but so far, the whole thing's just been one big pain in the ass!"

CHAPTER TWELVE

Aunt Olive had already gone back to their villa to shower and change for dinner, when Ellie finally left the Tiki Bar. The Beach Villa Wing consisted of a row of luxury suites which looked out onto the pool and had direct access to the deck via a private terrace. But the front doors of the villas faced the other direction and Ellie decided to go in that way, rather than via the sliding doors on the terrace. So she took the longer route which led through a couple of courtyards, before curving back past the front door of the villas.

Ellie had barely started walking, though, when she spotted Angela Brewer ahead of her. Instantly she thought of what Kelly and Melanie had just told her, and she quickened her steps to follow the woman. Angela marched out into a small parking lot on one side of the resort complex. Ellie watched as she walked up to a parked car and opened the trunk, then tried to heave a large case out. It was obviously heavy and Angela was struggling with it.

On an impulse, Elie hurried over and said: "Hi! You look like you're having trouble—would you like any help?"

Angela looked up and eyed Ellie suspiciously for a moment, then said: "Oh... you're the girl who was going to judge the Key Lime Pie Contest."

"Yes, that's me." Ellie gestured to the case again. "Do you want a hand with that?"

"Yeah, that would be great. Thanks."

"Oomph!" said Ellie as she took hold of one corner of the case and felt its weight. Together, she and Angela lifted the case out of the trunk and set it on the ground. "Whew! That was heavy! How long are you planning to stay?" Ellie asked jokingly.

"I wasn't planning to stay at the resort at all," retorted Angela. "If it weren't for the murder and the police wanting us to stay on site, I would have gone straight to my own condo after the contest. I've come down to Florida for the winter—I won't be heading back up north until March; that's why I've brought so much stuff. Still..." She glanced at the resort complex beside them. "It's a free stay at a luxury resort, so why not?" She looked back down at the huge case and added, "I wasn't even going to take my suitcase out—I've got an overnight bag with some stuff in there, which would have been fine for a few days. But then I realized that I packed most of my toiletries in this one. Do you mind waiting a minute while I get the stuff I need and then you can help me put it back in the car?"

"Oh sure, of course," said Ellie.

Angela knelt down beside her suitcase and fiddled with the combination, then opened it and began rummaging around. Ellie leaned against the side of the car and glanced idly inside the open trunk. There was a spare tire, a couple of reusable shopping bags, a car jack, and... Ellie caught her breath as she saw a large bottle tucked in the back corner. Was that antifreeze?

She glanced at Angela. The woman was still crouching on the ground, busily rummaging in her suitcase, and not paying Ellie any attention. Ellie leaned into the trunk to get a closer look at the bottle. Yes, her eyes hadn't deceived her: the label on the bottle had a picture of a skull with the words "*POISON: Ethylene Glycol*" underneath.

"What are you doing?" said a sharp voice behind her.

Ellie jumped and smacked her head against the lid of the trunk. "Oww!" She straightened, rubbing her head, and turned to find Angela scowling at her.

"Erm..." Ellie hesitated, not sure how to respond. Then she remembered that sometimes, offense was the best form of defense. "Is that a bottle of antifreeze?" she asked, pointing into the trunk.

Angela stiffened. "So what if it is?"

"Well, I just wondered why you would have it. Isn't

it too warm in Florida to need antifreeze?"

"It was in my car when I drove down from Michigan," said Angela. "And it's a myth that you don't need antifreeze in a warm climate. It's just called coolant down here. It's the same thing: ethylene glycol mixed with water. It stops water from freezing but it also raises the boiling point, which means it keeps the engine cool in a hot climate."

"Oh. Right," said Ellie.

She glanced back at the complex of buildings, mentally calculating the distance from this parking lot to the main parts of the resort. Was it just a coincidence that Angela should have a bottle of antifreeze in the trunk of her car, which was parked not that far away from the ballroom and the pavilion where they had been making their pies?

"I know what you're thinking," said Angela suddenly, glaring at Ellie. "You're thinking that I poisoned Chad Coleman, right? Just because I've got some antifreeze in my car?" She waved a hand around the parking lot. "You open the trunk of any of the cars here and I'll bet more than half of them will be carrying antifreeze. Tons of people have it in their cars. It doesn't make them criminals!"

"Yes, but most people weren't in the Key Lime Pie Contest and most didn't add extra whipped cream to their pie just before Chad Coleman tasted it," Ellie shot back.

"What? I don't know what you're talking about," said Angela, looking wary.

"I saw you," said Ellie. "You thought nobody was looking but I saw you take a piping bag out of your pocket and add some more whipped cream to the top of your pie."

"That's... that's because it got damaged!" said Angela defensively. "Whoever transported the pies knocked into mine and messed up the whipped cream topping. I'd spent forever making sure it looked *perfect* and then I saw that it was all smudged and squashed on one side. Well, I wasn't going to let some stupid waiter ruin my chances! I had to fix it!"

"How could you have known that your pie was going to get damaged?" asked Ellie skeptically. "Are you telling me that you always carry piping bags in your pocket, just in case?"

"Yeah," said Angela. "I always do that at competitions. I like to make sure that I've got something on me to do last-minute touch-ups." She scowled at Ellie. "Anyway, why would I have wanted to kill Chad Coleman? I barely knew him!"

"Well... maybe you didn't want him to ban you from the competition," said Ellie, repeating what Kelly had suggested. "You knew Coleman had a reputation for being tough with contestants and you always have to win every year, so you wanted to make sure that he didn't stand in your way."

"What—by killing off the judge? Yeah, that would really help me win," said Angela sarcastically. "Don't you think I would have at least waited to see who he announced as the winner first?"

Ellie flushed. Yes, Angela was right. It had been a stupid reason that didn't make any sense when you really looked at it. She had just been groping for some motive that she could pin on the woman.

"Anyway, if you suspect me just because I added a bit of whipped cream to my pie, then you should be totally jumping on Phil," said Angela.

"What d'you mean?"

"He added stuff to his pie too," said Angela. "Yeah. I saw him. It was while we were outside the ballroom, waiting to go in. This waiter came past us wheeling the cart with all the pies. The back doors to the ballroom were closed and Phil offered to push the cart while the waiter held the doors open. That seemed really sweet of him, right? Except that I saw what he did: he took a vial out of his pocket and sprinkled some stuff onto one of the pies. No one else saw him, 'cos he went in the ballroom first, pushing the cart, but I was right behind him and I saw it."

"What was he sprinkling on the pie?" asked Ellie.

Angela shrugged. "Beats me. It looked like some kind of white crystals." She slammed her suitcase shut again with a click and shouldered Ellie out of the way as she lifted it toward the trunk. "Now if you don't mind, I'd like to sort my stuff out and get back to my room."

Ellie wondered if she should offer to help lift the suitcase back into the trunk, but from the expression on Angela's face and the way the woman pointedly turned her back, she didn't think that Angela would accept her help anyway. With a sigh, Ellie turned and walked away.

Well, that first attempt at sleuthing didn't go well, thought Ellie as she continued on her way back to the villa. She felt a bit stupid for offering that lame motive as Angela's reason to kill Chad Coleman. Still, she reminded herself that she had picked up some interesting information: Angela carried a bottle of antifreeze in her car, which meant that she *did* have access to the same poison which had killed him. And whatever the woman might say, she had acted wary when questioned. *Of course, anyone might act wary when questioned about a murder,* Ellie admitted to herself. But she wasn't going to dismiss Angela Brewer just yet. There might still be some motive or connection between Angela and Coleman that she hadn't discovered.

And what about what Angela had said about Phil? Ellie frowned. Phil Garcia seemed like such a "nice guy," she just couldn't imagine him as some kind of murderer. But then, lots of murderers had fooled people before, hadn't they? There were always news stories about murderers who had seemed like perfectly nice and normal neighbors or husbands or fathers. Everyone was always shocked when it was revealed that they were cold-blooded killers.

Although Phil seems too soft and weak as well, thought Ellie. Then she reminded herself that poison was supposed to be a coward's weapon. So maybe it fit with Phil's profile perfectly!

CHAPTER THIRTEEN

"My goodness, poppet, I was just beginning to think I should send out a search party for you!" said Aunt Olive as Ellie let herself into the villa. "Where have you been? In fact, where have you been all day? I've hardly seen you!"

"I've been doing some sleuthing," said Ellie with a grin.

"Are you talking about Chad Coleman's murder?" Aunt Olive picked up a newspaper lying on the coffee table. "It's been all over the news today."

Ellie looked at what her aunt was holding: it was a local Tampa Bay paper and on the front page was a photo of Chad Coleman, with the headline: *"Local celebrity food critic murdered at Tampa Bay beach resort!"*

"What does it say about the police investigation?"

asked Ellie. "Have the police got any leads?"

"They're still convinced that Chef Marcel is the killer," said Aunt Olive. "I was chatting with some of the resort staff, and apparently the police have questioned Marcel several times, but he keeps insisting that he's innocent. And right now they haven't got anything on him. There's no evidence that he tampered with any of the pies. So they've had to let him go. He's back at work. The resort has stood behind him—"

"Yes, I know, Mr. Papadopoulos is personal friends with Chef Marcel and believes completely in his innocence," said Ellie. "That's the reason I've been so busy today." She told her aunt about the resort owner's request.

"So he's asked you to snoop around?" said Aunt Olive, her eyes sparkling. "How wonderful! Why didn't you tell me? I could have come and helped you! Solving a real-life murder mystery is so much better than writing one. So, what have you got planned next?"

"Next?" said Ellie blankly. "I don't know. I haven't really planned anything. I just thought tomorrow I'd do more of the same; you know, hang around the pool and see if I can pick up any gossip—"

"You're never going to solve any mystery doing that!" said Aunt Olive. "You've got to be proactive, dear. What about this other contestant, Phil? You haven't spoken to him, have you? And from what Angela said, he sounds very suspicious too."

"I haven't seen him all day—have you?" asked Ellie.

"I think I passed him when I was walking past *Hammerheads Bar and Grill.* He was sitting right in the back corner, with a book. I don't know why he was at a table inside—he's so pale, that boy! He needs to be out in the sun." Aunt Olive tutted. "And why was he sitting by himself? He should have been out by the pool. Lots of other young people there. He's a good-looking lad. I would have thought he would enjoy the company of some ladies."

"Maybe Phil is the shy type," suggested Ellie. "Remember how uncomfortable he was when that reporter woman was interviewing him in front of the cameras?"

"Hmmm... yes, now that you mention it, I do remember," said Aunt Olive with a gleam in her eye. "They asked him who he'd bring to the resort for a vacation and he said his mother."

"I thought that was very sweet," said Ellie.

"Oh, very sweet, but most grown men his age would probably be bringing a wife or a girlfriend... or boyfriend," added Aunt Olive with a wink. She looked thoughtfully down at the newspaper again. "Hmm... I'll bet he's a real 'mummy's boy.'" She picked the paper up and flipped eagerly to some pages inside. "They did an article highlighting each of the contestants... Ah, here it is! Yes, yes... just as I thought... Phil's photo shows him with his mother..."

Ellie looked at the paper, but she was more

interested in a photo at the bottom of the page. "That's her!" She grabbed the newspaper out of her aunt's hands and held it closer to her face. "That's the woman I saw that night outside the ballroom. And I saw her again when I was going to see Detective Carson. He said she's Coleman's wife, but he said she couldn't have been at the resort that night." Ellie paused and read the the caption beside the photo out loud:

"Chad was the love of my life!" a tearful Talisha Coleman said today. "He was an amazing man. There will be no one like him ever again. He was a talented cook, a charming TV personality, and a wonderful husband. I don't know what I'm going to do without him!"

"Well, apparently she's going to do very well without him," said Aunt Olive dryly. "I heard on the resort grapevine that she will inherit most of his estate; plus Coleman had a hefty life insurance policy, and Talisha Coleman is the sole beneficiary."

Ellie's eyes widened. "Really? Doesn't that make her the number one suspect?"

"Yes, but like you said, she has an alibi. She said she was at home on the night of the murder and the neighbors say that her car was in the driveway the entire time."

"She could have used another car or got in a taxi," said Ellie. "I'm positive I saw her that night, outside the back of the ballroom!"

"Didn't Detective Carson believe you?"

Ellie pulled a face. "No. He said he trusts his instincts and he believes that Talisha Coleman was telling him the truth. He thinks I might have been mistaken. Well, it *was* dark and I did only catch a fleeting glimpse of her face, but still..." She looked down at the photo again. "I'm sure it was her."

"You should trust your own instincts, dear," advised Aunt Olive. "I always do. The police are so often wrong... in life as well as in fiction! We can just do our own investigating without involving them." She glanced at her watch. "Now, you run along and change while I make a phone call to Mr. Papadopoulos."

"Why, what's the rush? I thought dinner wasn't until later."

"Yes, but I've organized a surprise for us before we go to dinner."

"A surprise?"

"Yes, we have a private demonstration on how to bake the perfect Key lime pie! I was chatting with Mr. Papadopoulos this afternoon and telling him how I was so inspired by the contest that I was thinking of including a Key lime pie in the story for my next book. I wanted to do some firsthand research on the best way to make it, just to be sure that my writing is authentic, and he offered to get Chef Marcel to give us a private demo."

Hmm, it would be a great opportunity to observe the man and ask him some questions too, thought Ellie. In spite of what Mr. Papadopoulos had said, she still wasn't quite ready to cross Chef Marcel off her list of suspects completely.

A short while later, they headed to the resort's "working kitchen." This was the place where most of the baking for all the different eateries was done. It was also where the resort's cooking workshops and demonstrations were held, and in fact, part of the kitchen was visible through a large display window, situated in a corridor just off the lobby. The outside of the glass display was decorated to look like a pretty balcony window in Europe, with wooden shutters on either side of the opening and a small ledge below, which held baskets of plastic geraniums. The wall around the display window was painted to give it a terracotta finish and the whole thing was very attractive. It was also one of the resort's attractions. Guests could watch the workshops in progress or the pastry chefs at work during the day. Children especially loved to press their noses against the glass pane and watch the pastry chefs rolling and kneading and mixing and frosting, as they made breads and pastries and muffins and cakes.

Ellie and Aunt Olive paused to look in the display window as they walked past. The enormous kitchen seemed to be empty, except for a man in the corner. He was wearing the traditional white chef's smock and had his back turned to them, but from the ginger hair and large, bulky build, Ellie guessed that it was Chef Marcel. He was bent over and seemed to be gesticulating at something near the ground.

They went through a door leading off the corridor and stepped into a small anteroom, with cubicles and hooks for guests to store their things before the workshops. As they were about to enter the kitchen itself, the door flew open and Mojito the resort cat ran out. Ellie and Aunt Olive had to duck to avoid a flying soup ladle which had obviously been thrown at the cat.

"*Casse toi, sale chat!*" bellowed a man's voice. "*Mon Dieu*, if I catch you in here again, I will roast you like a pig!"

CHAPTER FOURTEEN

Ellie and Aunt Olive exchanged a look, then pushed the swing doors open and cautiously poked their heads into the kitchen.

"Erm... hello? Chef Marcel?"

The Frenchman looked up, then beckoned them in impatiently. "Come in! Come in! But shut the door. I do not want that greedy beast in my kitchen again!"

Ellie and Aunt Olive hurried to do as they were told, then joined him at the workbench in the center of the room.

"Always, it is coming in here," he grumbled. "Always, looking for scraps on the counter, eh? Some chance to lick some cream, eh? *Alors...*" He put his big meaty hands on the counter and leaned toward them. "So you want to learn to make the Key lime pie?"

"Yes, I'm a writer, you see," Aunt Olive explained. "And I want to include it in the story for my next book. So it would be really helpful to see firsthand how it's made, by an expert, as well as learn a bit more about it. I heard that it was invented down in Key West?"

Chef Marcel nodded. "*Oui*. By the sponge divers. They were stuck on their boats for a long time, you know? And they have no fridge, so they can only have foods which do not spoil. Like crackers. And condensed milk. And Key limes. *Et voila!*" He made a twirling motion with his hand. "The Key lime pie is born. They did not even bake it, you know. They have no ovens. But mixing the ingredients is enough. It is a chemical reaction, between the acid in the lime juice and the protein in the milk and eggs."

"Wow, that's fascinating," said Aunt Olive. "So why do we bake the pies now?"

Chef Marcel shrugged. "It is like this for many things. We have become *le sissy*, you know? Always scared of everything. People do not want to eat anything with raw eggs these days."

"What about the color?" asked Ellie. "I don't know why but I always thought Key lime pie would be green. I was really surprised when I was served my first slice and it turned out to be yellow."

"Bah! The pie must never be green!" growled Chef Marcel. "It is wrong! Wrong! That is food coloring. A real Key lime pie is always yellow, like the fruit." He indicated a few small citrus fruits on the counter in front of them.

Ellie reached out to pick up a Key lime and turned it over curiously. It was a lot smaller than the limes she was used to and the skin was a pale yellow, rather than glossy green. She held it up to her nose and sniffed it. It did have a strong aromatic fragrance.

"*Tiens,* I have prepared for you to make your own pie," said Chef Marcel, indicating the group of supplies on the counter. "The best way to learn and experience is to do it yourself."

"Oh yes, that's a brilliant idea," said Aunt Olive, rolling up her sleeves.

For the next hour, Ellie and Aunt Olive followed Chef Marcel's instructions as they pounded the graham crackers into a loose crumb, then mixed it with butter and pressed it into the bottom of a shallow pie dish. When that was done, they each put their dishes into a large industrial oven to bake while they started on the filling. Ellie watched Chef Marcel expertly crack eggs and separate the yolk from the white, and she tried to copy him. They added condensed milk to the egg yolks, and then the star ingredient: the freshly squeezed Key lime juice.

"*Allez! Allez!* Mix, quickly!" Chef Marcel urged them, demonstrating with a whisk.

Ellie and Aunt Olive both stirred their mixtures briskly. Ellie got so excited when she saw her mixture begin to thicken that she completely forgot about the mystery of Chad Coleman's murder for a few moments.

"Oh! It's happening! It's happening!" she cried.

"*Bien*," said Chef Marcel, looking approvingly at her bowl. He pointed at the pie dishes, which had been taken out of the oven and had been cooling on the side. "It is almost ready to fill the pies. You just need to make the topping now."

Aunt Olive decided to make hers with the most commonly served whipped cream topping, but Ellie decided to go with the so-called "traditional" meringue topping instead. Her heart sank, though, when Chef Marcel handed her a hand whisk.

"Can't I use a machine?" asked Ellie in dismay.

Chef Marcel glowered at her. "*Non*. By hand is the best way."

Ellie sighed and got to work. By the time the egg whites and sugar had been beaten into stiff peaks, she felt like her arms were going to fall off!

"Hah! You should have gone with the easy route," gloated Aunt Olive, brandishing a can of ready-made, pressurized whipped cream.

"Mine will taste much better," Ellie retorted as she massaged her aching biceps.

They filled their respective pie cases with their fillings, and then placed the pies in the oven.

"Twenty minutes," said Chef Marcel, glancing at his watch. "Then you can add the meringue to one and put it back in the oven for browning. After that, they will both need to go in the chiller cabinet for cooling, before you can add the whipped cream topping."

"In the chiller?" said Ellie, dismayed. "For how long?"

"A couple of hours at least."

"Ohhh... I was hoping to taste them immediately."

"Ah, *non, non,*" said Chef Marcel, wagging a finger. "They must be chilled for the maximum flavor. You can come back and taste them after dinner. *Bon*, I must go to my office for a few minutes to make some phone calls. You are OK here? I will come back to check on the pies and help you put them in the chiller."

Aunt Olive sat down on a stool after he'd left and began writing notes in a notebook, but Ellie wandered restlessly around the kitchen. She was impatient for the pies to be done and she chafed at the extra delay of having to chill them. As she wandered down to the other end of the huge kitchen, she saw an enormous glass chiller cabinet. It had several shelves inside with various desserts, fresh fruit mixes and compotes, lumps of dough in plastic wrap, jugs of cream, and other things being refrigerated.

Next to the chiller, Ellie noticed a thick metal door with a sign that had the symbol of a snowflake on it. Curious, she pulled on the handle and the heavy door swung open to reveal a walk-in freezer. A cloud of icy air wafted out.

"Aunt Olive—look at this freezer! It's enormous!" said Ellie.

"Mm-hmm," said Aunt Olive, her head down as she scribbled in her notebook.

"Hey, you know what? Why don't we put our pies in here, rather than the chiller? Wouldn't that cool them down a lot faster?"

Aunt Olive didn't answer, still engrossed in making her notes. Ellie hesitated, then walked into the freezer. It was like a giant walk-in pantry. She wandered farther in, marveling at all the items neatly stacked on the shelves or hanging from hooks attached to the ceiling. There were frozen meat, fish, soup stock, berries, ice-cream, and more.

Ellie looked around for a good place to put her pie. Most of the shelves were full, but she noticed a shelf in the far corner which might have space. It was the highest shelf on that wall and seemed to hold nothing other than a big bag of ice. She was sure that if she shoved the bag farther in, there would be enough space on the shelf for her to prop her pie on the edge. Ellie reached up and tried to push the bag, but it resisted. It felt like there was something behind it. Frowning, she pulled the bag down to see what was there. It looked like a bulky square package of some kind, wrapped in layers of plastic.

What is that? Ellie was just about to reach up to pull the package down when a step sounded behind her and a voice snapped:

"*Zut!* DO NOT TOUCH THAT!"

CHAPTER FIFTEEN

Ellie gasped and whirled around. Chef Marcel was standing behind her, his face dark with anger.

"What are you doing in here?" he demanded. He hustled her out of the freezer and shut the door firmly behind them. "You were snooping, eh? In my freezer?"

It sounded so ridiculous that Ellie almost laughed. "I wasn't snooping," she said. "I was just looking for a place to put my pie."

"I told you to put the pies in the chiller, not the freezer."

"Yes, I know. I just thought the freezer would be quicker. You know, cool it down faster."

"I'm sure Ellie meant no harm," said Aunt Olive, coming to stand behind her niece.

"A good cook does not just care about fast-fast-

fast," snapped Chef Marcel, snapping his fingers to emphasize each "fast." "I tell you to put in the chiller and that is what you should do! You listen to me!"

"Bloody hell... I'm sorry," muttered Ellie.

She was taken aback by Marcel's change in manner. Instead of the friendly, benevolent teacher that he had been for the last hour, he was suddenly a cold, hard-eyed stranger.

As if he was suddenly aware of the change himself, Marcel's manner softened and he added gruffly, "*Alors*, I do not mean to lose my temper but it is because I am worried. The freezer door—it has been giving trouble for many days. There is a problem with the safety knob. I have called the resort technicians but they have not fixed it yet. I do not want you to be locked inside by mistake."

Huh. A likely story, thought Ellie. It was obviously a lame excuse for his unreasonably aggressive reaction. Still, she didn't argue. Instead, she followed Marcel silently back to the other side of the kitchen and watched as he stomped over to the ovens and took their pies out. They spent several minutes making stilted conversation as they waited for the pies to cool down enough to be placed in the chiller. Once the pies were on the chiller cabinet shelf, Marcel could barely wait for them to leave. He rushed them out of the kitchen, saying: "You must excuse me now. I am very busy. I will tell someone to bring the pies to you after you finish your dinner. Good night."—before leaving them in the lobby and disappearing into the resort's inner offices.

Ellie followed her aunt as they walked slowly back to their villa. She kept thinking about Chef Marcel's reaction and after a few minutes, she burst out:

"Don't you think that was a bit of an extreme reaction? I mean, I just walked into his freezer, for heaven's sake! He acted like I'd broken into an underground vault in a bank or something."

"Ah well, you know how temperamental these chef types can be," said Aunt Olive. "I think he was angry that you didn't follow his instructions. Men like Marcel can't bear to be disobeyed. When I was chatting with the resort staff about him, they all said he has a terrible temper, yelling and throwing things. Look how he reacted to that silly cat! I imagine it must be a nightmare working in his kitchen. I'd hate to be one of his sous-chefs!"

"Hmm…" said Ellie thoughtfully. She wasn't convinced that Chef Marcel's behavior had just been fueled by anger. She was sure that she had also seen fear in his eyes. *But what had he been scared of?* Then it dawned on her. *Of course!* He had accused her of snooping in the freezer. It was a ridiculous thing to say—it's why she had thought it was funny at the time. But now she realized that it suggested something else: why would he care that anyone was "snooping in his freezer" unless there was something there he didn't want anyone to see? That must have been why he got so angry and bundled her out so quickly. He had been afraid that she might have seen or found something in there that she shouldn't.

That square package behind the bag of ice! thought Ellie. *What's in it?* She was sure that that was what Chef Marcel was hiding. She wished now that she'd had a chance to take it down and look inside. She wondered if there was a way she could return to that kitchen and get back inside the freezer for another look.

"*MIAOW!*"

Ellie looked down and saw that Mojito had materialized out of the greenery surrounding the path they were on. The resort cat's black fur shimmered in the light of the nearby lamp and her green eyes glittered like emeralds. Ellie bent down to stroke her.

"What's Chef Marcel hiding in his freezer, eh?" she said to the cat. "I'll bet you know. Cats always know everything."

"I wonder how she got into the kitchen?" mused Aunt Olive. "I got the impression from the way Chef Marcel reacted that it's something that's happened often. You'd think he would make sure Mojito can't get in through the door, and yet it sounded like she'd been making a regular nuisance of herself."

"*MIAOW!*" said Mojito indignantly, turning her unblinking green stare on Aunt Olive.

Ellie laughed. "I don't think she liked you calling her a nuisance! Still, I do wish I could speak 'cat' sometimes. Mojito seems to get into all sorts of places in the resort and I'll bet she could give me all sorts of clues to the case."

The next morning, Ellie was woken by Aunt Olive shaking her shoulder excitedly and saying: "Get up, poppet! It's a beautiful morning! Come on, we're going to be late."

"Late for what?" mumbled Ellie, sitting up slowly in bed and yawning. She rubbed her eyes, then glanced at the clock on her bedside table and groaned. "Aunt Olive! It's not even eight o'clock! Why are we getting up so early?"

"Because we need to get down to the beach," Aunt Olive said.

"Huh? You're the one who always says 'there should be a law passed so that no business is conducted before ten o'clock and a decent cup of tea'... I can't believe you want to go on an early morning beach walk now!"

"Not a walk," said her aunt impatiently. "Beach yoga for ladies! It's one of the resort activities on offer. Wouldn't it be a shame not to take part in it?"

Ellie looked at her aunt incredulously. "Since when are you so keen to join in resort activities at eight in the morning?"

"You'll see," said Aunt Olive mysteriously. "Well, come on, poppet! I thought you came to Florida to learn new things, try new experiences! Are you chickening out now?"

"No, but—"

"Then hurry and get dressed, dear, or we'll miss the beginning of class!"

CHAPTER SIXTEEN

Twenty minutes later, a slightly bewildered and still very sleepy Ellie followed her aunt out onto the private beach area owned by the Sunset Palms Beach Resort. A young woman in skintight leggings and a pink neon crop top was standing in front of a group of people spread out on the sand. Everyone had a yoga mat unrolled in front of them and Ellie was glad that the resort staff had provided her and her aunt with mats. She gripped it tightly now as they joined the group. She had never done yoga before and in spite of her grumbling to her aunt, she was secretly excited. She had seen photos of people doing morning yoga on beautiful beaches. It always looked so serene and idyllic, and wonderfully relaxing. She had dreamed of being able to join a class like that.

This is going to be amazing, Ellie thought, smiling

to herself. She was sure that she was going to be a natural and would flow gracefully into each yoga pose, while achieving the perfect rhythm of Zen breathing.

Aunt Olive had made a beeline for a spot at the front, next to a gray-haired lady who looked vaguely familiar. There was no space next to them for another mat, so Ellie chose a spot at the rear of the group and unrolled her mat on the sand. She was just sitting down cross-legged and trying to place her hands in the lotus position when a shadow fell over her.

"*Namaste.*" A woman pressed her palms together and bowed to Ellie.

"Oh... erm... hi," said Ellie, smiling uncertainly at her.

The woman twitched. "So, like, you're in my spot."

"Your spot?"

"Yeah, I always have that corner in class."

"Oh." Ellie looked around at the empty expanse of sand around them. "But... we're not in a room."

"That's my spot," the woman insisted. "I need to be there when I practice. It's important for the flow of my energy channels. Otherwise I'll feel totally blocked if I'm cramped."

"But..." Ellie looked in puzzlement again at the open beach around them. "Can't you just put your mat here, next to me? We've got the whole beach. What difference does a few feet make?"

The woman's face was turning red. "Of course it makes a difference! That is one of the goals of yoga—

to achieve balance and enable the free flow of Zen spirit. You're blocking my *chi*. You're preventing me from reaching karmic fulfilment."

"Erm... OK..." said Ellie, giving the woman a weird look. She scooted her mat a few feet away.

The woman huffed. "Not there either."

"What? Why not?" asked Ellie impatiently.

The woman gestured to the sun in the sky. "Can't you see? You're in the path of the sun's rays. You're shadowing me from its healing warmth!"

Ellie was starting to lose her temper. "The sun is above our heads now. I'm not blocking anything."

"Yes, you are! You're blocking the energy channels I need to achieve peace in my poses. Especially now when I need it so much." The woman's face creased with sorrow. "The sadness, the suffering I have had to endure since losing Lorenzo."

"Oh." Ellie softened her tone. She felt bad suddenly. If the woman had recently lost her partner, maybe she could be excused for behaving unreasonably. "Erm... I'm sorry. I didn't realize."

"Nobody realizes the anguish I feel!" the woman cried, pressing a hand to her heart. "No one thought much of Lorenzo, just because he wasn't very big— and OK, I admit, he also didn't talk much. But he was there for me, every day, for the last ten years." She gave Ellie a sulky look. "Anyway, it's not true that Lorenzo didn't talk. Most people just didn't understand him. But I'm sure when he was blowing bubbles, he was telling me that he loved me."

"Wait—what? Blowing bubbles?" Ellie stared at the woman. "Who is Lorenzo again?"

"My goldfish."

"You want me to move my mat so you can achieve inner peace or whatever over your dead goldfish?" said Ellie.

The woman gave a scandalized gasp. "Wow. That is so insensitive!" She put up a hand, palm out, toward Ellie. "I just... I can't deal with this right now. I'm not going to engage with you anymore." She sat down, cross-legged, on her mat, and began breathing noisily in and out of her mouth while humming: "*Soooooo... Huuuuuuum....*"

Ellie stared at the woman in disbelief for a moment. OK, on second thought, she wasn't sure she wanted to do yoga next to such a nutcase anyway. She gathered up her mat and moved to the other side of the group. As she unrolled it, the teacher stepped forward and raised her arms, smiling at the group.

"*Namaste.* Welcome, all of you, to this morning's session of beach yoga! Now, everybody on your mats... we're going to start with some Sun Salutations... Yes, take a deep inhale... arms up to the sky... folding forward... strong backs... good... now coming up into a Downward-Facing Dog..."

"Ungh!" Ellie grunted as she struggled to get her legs straight and her buttocks in the air.

Somehow, beach yoga wasn't turning out to be as easy or as serene as she thought. Her muscles screamed with every stretch and she was humiliated to find that she kept falling over every time she tried to stand on one leg. Ellie sneaked a glance at the rest of the class. How did everyone else make it look so easy and effortless? Even Aunt Olive was bending and stretching gracefully through every pose!

By the time the class was finished, Ellie was panting with effort and sore in several places. And she had never felt less relaxed in her life! She staggered to her feet and went over to join Aunt Olive, who was rolling up her mat. As her aunt turned, she made a great show of pausing and doing a double take. Then Aunt Olive gave an exaggerated gasp and said to the gray-haired lady on the mat next to her:

"You're Phil Garcia's mother, aren't you?"

The woman looked up in surprise. "Yes, I'm Dolores Garcia. But how did you know—"

"Oh, I recognize you from the photo in the papers," said Aunt Olive. "And of course, Phil's told me all about you."

"He... he has?"

"Oh yes, he and I had a lovely chat yesterday. I think he was feeling a bit lonely, you know? I'm sure I reminded him in some way of you," Aunt Olive said blithely, ignoring the fact that she was several pounds heavier, wearing a rainbow yoga outfit, heavy mascara and lipstick, and looked nothing like the dowdy, skinny woman next to her. "I do think young men appreciate having a maternal figure around, even if they don't want to admit it—don't you think? And we had such a nice chat. Phil told me that he'd wanted to win the contest so that he could bring you here for a vacation."

"Yes, Phil is such a good boy. So gentle, so thoughtful," Dolores Garcia murmured.

"And such a good teacher too, I hear," said Aunt Olive archly. "You must be so proud of him."

"Oh yes, especially after what he's been through, everything that he's suffered—but he never complains."

"What happened to him?" asked Aunt Olive.

"Poor Phil got a terrible case of food poisoning. It put him in the hospital for weeks and it's left him suffering from IBS—you know, irritable bowel syndrome—ever since. He had to be off work for months and he'd been up for a promotion, you know. He was going to be the head of his department. But instead, he lost his teaching job." Dolores shook her head. "Of course, he's back to teaching now, but only as a substitute teacher and the pay isn't as good as a regular position, plus there's no security."

"Oh, how dreadful!" cried Aunt Olive. "The poor dear! How did this happen? Did he have some dodgy seafood or something?"

"Dodgy?" Dolores looked at Aunt Olive blankly.

"Oh, that's a British expression," Aunt Olive explained. "It means poor quality or unreliable, or even dishonest if you're talking about a person."

"Ah. Well, it was a little strange." Dolores frowned. "It shouldn't have been... er... 'dodgy,' as you say. We were eating at this super fancy Italian restaurant that Phil took me to for my birthday. Over in downtown St. Pete. So you'd think the food would be safe. And it was recommended too—that's why Phil chose the place. It was Chad Coleman, actually, who gave it an awesome review in the local papers."

"Chad Coleman?" cried Ellie.

Dolores Garcia nodded. "Yes, Mr. Coleman specifically recommended their seafood spaghetti, so that's what Phil ordered." She sighed. "I guess he was just mighty unlucky."

"Oh dear!" Aunt Olive clucked her tongue. "He must be very angry and bitter about the whole thing.'

"Oh no, not Phil," said Dolores quickly. "He's such a sweetie, he never holds grudges. No matter how badly he's been treated or taken advantage of, he always looks on the bright side of things." She smiled proudly. "He's always been like that, ever since he was a little boy. Phil is the nicest, most kind and generous guy. I always say that he'll make a lucky woman a great husband some day!"

"Ah, does he have a lucky woman in mind?" asked Aunt Olive with a coy smile.

Dolores Garcia looked mournful. "No, the girls don't seem to appreciate Phil. I don't know what it is. He's never had a serious girlfriend. I suppose he's a bit shy; he doesn't quite know how to talk to the ladies." She turned suddenly to Ellie and gave her a speculative look. "Have you met Phil?"

"Me? Oh... erm... yes, just briefly," said Ellie, not liking the gleam in the woman's eyes.

"Well! We must introduce you properly," said Dolores eagerly. "I'm sure the two of you would hit it off! Phil could even take you sightseeing around Tampa—"

"Oh...uh... that's really nice of you to offer, Mrs. Garcia, but... erm... I'm sure Phil is too busy with his schoolwork and stuff," said Ellie hastily.

A few minutes later, after they'd bade farewell to Phil's mother and walked away, she said under her breath: "Whew! If we'd stayed talking any longer, Dolores Garcia would have become my mother-in-law!"

Aunt Olive burst out laughing. "Well, as someone who married a Yank, I can recommend the experience." She gave her niece a sly look. "And I get the impression that there's a certain handsome American doctor who's caught your eye?"

"What? Rubbish!" said Ellie, feeling her cheeks getting warm. Quickly, she changed the subject. "How did you know that Phil's mother would be at the yoga class?"

"Because I arranged for her to be there. I spoke to Mr. Papadopoulos last night while you were showering and changing for dinner. I asked him to send Phil's mother a special invitation to come and enjoy the amenities at the resort while her son is here. In particular, I told him to urge her to join the morning beach yoga class." Aunt Olive smiled complacently. "Of course, Dolores has no idea that I had anything to do with it. She just thinks that the resort is being very kind and generous to give her a free vacation with her son."

"And you never had a cozy chat with Phil yesterday, did you? You made all that up," said Ellie accusingly.

Aunt Olive looked unrepentant. "Well, I *could* have had a chat with him," she said. "I needed a way to get Dolores Garcia to open up and the easiest way to butter up most parents is to gush about their children."

"You're devious," said Ellie, shaking her head.

Aunt Olive grinned "I'll take that as a compliment."

"Still, it was clever because we now know that Phil Garcia could have had a motive," said Ellie eagerly.

"Now, don't get carried away, poppet," said Aunt Olive. "Just because the man got food poisoning at a restaurant that Chad Coleman recommended doesn't mean that he would want to kill Coleman. It's a pretty far-fetched motive!"

"Yes, but it wasn't just a bit of vomiting and diarrhea, was it?" argued Ellie. "It sounds like Phil lost months of his life to the illness and it cost him his career too. Those are more than enough reasons to feel bitter. And especially when you consider what Angela told me, about seeing him add something to one of the pies—"

"Ah, now, I've been thinking about that," said Aunt Olive. "You do know that ethylene glycol is a liquid? Whereas Angela said she saw Phil sprinkle solid white crystals."

"Maybe it was some other kind of poison," Ellie suggested.

Aunt Olive shook her head. "The autopsy report confirmed that Chad Coleman died of ethylene glycol poisoning."

Ellie blew out a breath of frustration. "This case just keeps getting more and more puzzling!"

CHAPTER SEVENTEEN

After breakfast, Aunt Olive went off to have a facial treatment at the resort spa, leaving Ellie to her own devices. She changed into her bikini and wandered down to the pool. She was determined to give the whole "swimming" thing another go. *But maybe it's time I enlisted help*, she admitted. *Something to give me the confidence that I won't just sink and drown in the water.*

So she took a deep breath and marched herself across the pool deck to the kiosk which supplied flotation devices and other pool toys to the guests. She eyed the range of things on offer. Oh no, she couldn't bear the humiliation of wearing armbands like a toddler! And the giant inflatable killer whale and other pool floats were all too conspicuous. As for a paddle board... ugh, she'd feel like she was back in those awful school swimming classes with the scary teacher who used to stand at the edge of the pool and glare at her while blowing on a whistle... and the water was always freezing... and the changing rooms damp and cold, with cramped wooden cubicles and the smell of chlorine everywhere...

Ellie was so lost in her thoughts that she didn't notice the young man coming up beside her. Then she heard someone clearing their throat and she turned to find Phil Garcia standing next to her.

"Oh!" She was so surprised to see him, especially after all the speculation about him, that she was struck dumb for a moment.

"Hi," he said, smiling shyly. "Uh... I recognize you. You're the girl who was going to judge us in the second round of the contest, right?"

"Yes, that's me. My name's Ellie Bishop. And you're Phil, aren't you?"

He nodded, then shifted from foot to foot, looking excruciatingly embarrassed. Ellie wondered if his mother had put him up to this. Suddenly, she felt sorry for him. Giving him a friendly smile, she said, "Erm... I don't suppose you could recommend a flotation device? I can't swim."

"Oh." Phil looked a bit more relaxed. "Sure. Yeah, it really helps to have something that keeps you afloat. Gives you confidence in the water." He bent to pick up a long polystyrene tube bent in a U-shape. "How about a pool noodle? They're awesome. You can put them around your chest if you want to swim forward or behind you, like, under your armpits, if you want to sit back in the water. They really help you stay afloat."

Ellie noticed that Phil's manner had changed, now that he was distracted and not focusing on himself. The shy, stammering young man was gone, to be replaced by a patient, knowledgeable teacher. *He's actually not bad looking, when he's not hunching his shoulders and looking down all the time*, thought Ellie. *If he just projected a bit more confidence, I'll bet Phil could be really attractive to the ladies.*

"Thanks," she said, taking the noodle and examining it. "This doesn't look too childish."

"Yes, it's very popular with adults," said Phil. "In fact, people use them for water therapy and rehab, you know. My physical therapist used some when he was working with me."

Ellie looked at him curiously. "Physical therapy? Were you in an accident?"

"Oh, no." Phil flushed. "I... uh... I ended up in the hospital with severe food poisoning. I was in bed for weeks and when I finally recovered, my muscles were really weak. I had to do some physical therapy to get back into shape."

"Gosh, that sounds awful," said Ellie, making a sympathetic face.

Phil shrugged. "It wasn't great. But I guess it could have been worse. I heard some people with food poisoning end up with permanent organ failure and stuff."

"Still, it must have been really disruptive to your life. I mean, to be hospitalized for weeks!"

"Yeah. That was bad. And I do still have some... uh... digestion issues, and I find that a lot of the stuff you buy in stores has additives and things which trigger my problems. That was why I started learning to bake, you know, so I could make sure I knew exactly what I was eating. Then I found that it was really relaxing too!" He beamed at her.

Ellie looked at the nice young man in front of her and just couldn't believe that he could be a murderer. But what about the things Angela had said? Had the older woman been lying when she said she saw Phil furtively add something to the pies? Ellie half-wished that she could just come out and ask Phil bluntly: *"What did you add to that pie?"* But of course she couldn't do that, standing here, chatting by the pool...

"MIAOW! MIAOW!"

Ellie looked down to see that Mojito the resort cat had suddenly decided to join them. She was standing next to Ellie's legs and rubbing her chin on the edge of a giant inflatable lobster.

"MIAOW!" she said again, looking up at them.

"Oh!" Phil hastily stepped back and began edging away from the cat.

This, of course, made Mojito instantly more interested in him. Cats always seemed to gravitate toward the one person in the room who wanted nothing to do with them! She strolled toward Phil and began to rub her body against his ankles.

"Nooo... no, no!" cried Phil.

Then he began to sneeze. Ellie watched in amazement as he sneezed and sneezed and sneezed.

"Erm... Are you okay?" she asked, putting a hand out to him.

"I'm... *ahh... aahh... AHHTCHOO!* ...I'm allergic to cats," he said in a muffled voice as he clutched his nose.

His face was beginning to get red and puffy, and his eyes were streaming. He tried to move away again, but Mojito obviously thought this was a great new game. She trotted after Phil and jumped up on a lounge chair next to him, so that she was higher up and closer to his face.

"*MIAOW!*" she said, rubbing herself against his hip.

"*AHHTCHOO... AHHTCHOO!*" sneezed Phil, doubling over. Then he clutched his back suddenly and cried out in pain. The sound scared Mojito and she jumped off the lounge and ran away.

"What is it?" asked Ellie, reaching out to support Phil.

"My... my back," he groaned. "Ohhh... it's killing me!"

Ellie helped him hobble to the nearby lounge, but when he tried to sit down, he gasped and cried out in pain once more.

"You need to see a doctor," Ellie said. "Come on, I'll take you to the resort clinic. I'm sure Blake—I mean, Dr. Thornton will be able to help you."

Phil grimaced and nodded. He slung an arm over Ellie's shoulder and she supported him as they made their way slowly and painfully across the pool deck. They went through the courtyard behind the main resort building, then took the path that led to many of the resort offices. Ellie was relieved to see that there was no one in the waiting room outside Blake's office and they found the doctor himself sitting at his desk, dictating some notes.

"Ellie!" He sprang up with a smile when he saw her, then his face sobered as he saw Phil. "What happened?"

Ellie explained quickly while Blake helped Phil onto the examination bed.

"Do you think he's broken his back?" she asked Blake anxiously.

"I doubt it. He wouldn't be able to stand up if that was the case. No, what's more likely is that the muscles in his back have gone into a spasm." Blake looked at Phil. "Do you normally suffer from a bad back?"

Phil nodded. "Yeah. I always get backaches. Must be all those years hunched over, grading papers," he said with a wry laugh. "The physical therapist told me that I have a really weak lumbar spine."

Blake nodded. "It's a common problem. You need to work on strengthening your core muscles. Now, I'm going to give you some anti-inflammatories and some fast-acting painkillers. Are you allergic to any medication?"

"I don't think so." Phil grimaced with pain. "Just give me whatever you've got, doc!"

CHAPTER EIGHTEEN

Ellie watched Blake expertly draw liquid from a vial into a syringe and then inject it into the muscles in Phil's lower back. He also gave the young teacher some painkillers to swallow, as well as an antihistamine to help reduce the swelling from his allergy. She hovered uncertainly next to them, not sure what to do. She felt a bit intrusive standing there but, at the same time, she was the one who had brought Phil and she felt bad just abandoning him. She was wondering whether to speak up and offer to leave when they heard a voice in the waiting room outside.

"Hey doc! Can you come quick? One of the kids in the Pirate Playground is having a bad nosebleed and the parents are freaking out."

Blake glanced at Ellie. "Do you mind staying with

Phil for a while? I've just given him some strong painkillers and I don't want to leave him alone."

"Oh, sure. As long as I don't have to do any actual doctoring," she said jokingly.

Blake went out, leaving them alone in the cool examination room. Ellie perched on a chair next to the bed and watched Phil, whose pain seemed to be finally easing.

"Are you feeling better?" she asked.

"Yeah, much better," he sighed. Then to Ellie surprise, he giggled. "Who would have thought I'd end up here all because of a kitty cat... kitty kitty kitty..." He giggled again.

Ellie eyed him worriedly. Phil sounded a bit like he was drunk... or high... or a mixture of both. His voice was slurred and he had a silly smile on his face.

"Erm... are you OK?" she asked him.

"Sure, having a great time!" he said. "This is just like that ride at Disney World... you know, the teacups in the Mad Tea Party... spinning... spinning... spinning around... Wheee!" He whooped and tried to get off the bed.

"Whoa!" Ellie sprang up and forced him to lie back down. "OK, I think those painkillers are beginning to work a bit too well," she said with a laugh. Trying to distract him, she said, "So... erm... Phil, you must be really gutted about the contest. I know you were hoping to bring your mother here for her sixtieth birthday."

He frowned at her. "Gutted? I wasn't gutted." He

127

patted his stomach and giggled. "I've got all my guts right here!"

Ellie chuckled. "Sorry, it's a British expression. It means, like, really disappointed or devastated."

"Oh, yeah, sure. I really wanted to win. I practiced my Key lime pie recipe over and over again at home, just so I would have it perfect on the day."

"Did your recipe have any unusual ingredients?" asked Ellie casually.

"No, pretty much the usual things: eggs, condensed milk, Key lime juice... We had to use whatever was at our workstations. We weren't allowed to bring stuff from home, you know."

"But I don't understand—if you all used the same ingredients, how did you end up with variations in your pies?"

"Oh, we could ask for extra stuff and the resort would provide it. Like, I asked for vanilla extract to mix into my graham cracker mixture. Some of the others asked for nuts to mix in with the graham crackers or cream cheese to add to the filling."

Hmm... so this means it would have been really difficult for any contestant to add the poison to the pie during the baking stage since all the ingredients would have come from the resort, thought Ellie. *The most likely opportunity they would've had was after the pies were done. But unless they had access to the chiller where all the pies were being kept, they could only do any tampering in that small window of opportunity when the pies were being transported to the ballroom and placed on the trestle table, before judging began.*

Which is exactly what Angela said Phil had done, Ellie reminded herself. The other woman claimed to have seen him sprinkling white crystals on one of the pies just when they were being transported into the ballroom. Ellie glanced back at the young man lying on the bed next to her. He was now staring at the ceiling and humming: "Vanilla-nilla-nilla..." and giggling to himself. He looked so sweet and silly, she just couldn't imagine him as a killer!

But a good sleuth doesn't let her emotions get in the way, Ellie reminded herself. She took a deep breath and said, in a harder voice:

"You didn't just use the resort ingredients in your pie, though, did you, Phil? You brought something from home which you secretly added just before the judging."

Phil stopped humming and looked at her in alarm. "What... what are you talking about?"

"You pretended to help the waiter who was pushing the cart with the pies into the ballroom and you secretly sprinkled some stuff on top of one of the pies."

Phil licked his lips. "No... I... I didn't—"

"Someone saw you do it," said Ellie.

Phil went pale. "I... it wasn't—"

"It was a clever way to add poison to a pie—"

"Wait—*what?*" cried Phil. "*Poison?* You think I'm the one who poisoned Chad Coleman?"

"Aren't you?" Ellie said. "What was the stuff you sprinkled on the pie?"

"It wasn't poison!" cried Phil, looking horrified. "Why would you think I'd want to kill Chad Coleman? I don't have any beef with him."

"You wanted to get back at him."

"For what?"

"For giving you food poisoning."

"Huh?" Phil looked completely confused.

"Well, indirectly," said Ellie. "Chad Coleman recommended the restaurant and even the dish which gave you the food poisoning. So you probably blamed him for destroying your career and ruining your life."

"*What?*" Phil struggled to sit up in the bed. "Are you nuts? That's the craziest, stupidest motive I've ever heard of! You think I would murder someone just because he recommended a restaurant where I got food poisoning?" He shook his head. "First of all, I could never kill anyone! But even if I could, don't you think it would make more sense for me to murder the owner of the restaurant who actually gave me the food?"

Ellie hesitated. Now that he put it like that, she could see that it *was* a pretty lame motive. Still, she wasn't willing to give up just yet.

"Well, if it wasn't poison, then what was it?" she demanded. "You definitely added *something* to one of the pies on the sly."

Phil looked slightly ashamed. "It was monosodium

glutamate."

"What's that?"

"It's a flavor enhancer. You ever heard of MSG? People always think of Chinese restaurants, but actually, MSG is often added to cakes and things, you know, to make them taste better. It sort of intensifies the flavors and makes things taste creamier."

"Well, if it's so innocent, how come you were trying to hide it?"

Phil looked down and fidgeted with his hands. "I guess it *was* sort of cheating. That's why I didn't want anyone to see me. But I'd heard that Chad Coleman could be a super tough judge, so I desperately wanted to have something to help my pie stand out. But it wasn't poison!" he insisted. "I've still got some MSG in my room. I can eat some in front of you, if you want, to prove it!"

"That's OK," said Ellie, believing him. She was beginning to feel bad about getting him so agitated.

"You're not gonna tell anyone, are you?" asked Phil anxiously. "Especially not my mother! She'd be so upset if she found out. She's got really high standards for me and I'd hate to let her down. Please?"

CHAPTER NINETEEN

Ellie hesitated. She knew she shouldn't make a promise to stay silent; instead, she should've gone to the police with any new details. Even if Phil hadn't added anything poisonous to his pie, the information might've still been valuable for the investigation. But as she looked at his pleading puppy-dog eyes, she felt herself caving.

"All right, I won't say anything."

"Oh, man, thanks so much!" cried Phil, grabbing her hand and pumping it up and down. Then he realized what he was doing and let go, blushing. "Sorry. I didn't mean—"

The door to the clinic flew open and Kelly Nguyen rushed in. She was wearing a pink dress with thin spaghetti straps that left her shoulders bare, and carrying a beach tote. Her long black hair was pulled back in a sleek ponytail and she looked incredibly pretty. She glanced around the empty waiting area, then came into Blake's office.

"Oh!" she said as she saw Ellie and Phil. "Sorry, I was looking for the doctor."

"He's just been called to one of the playgrounds, but he should be back soon," said Ellie.

Kelly sank into a chair next to them with a sigh. "Good, I really need him to look at my shoulders." She turned to display her bare shoulders and Ellie recoiled at the sight of the red, blistering skin.

"Bloody hell—what happened to you?" she cried.

Phil leaned over to look, then said, "It looks like sunburn. Did you go out without sunscreen?"

"Yeah, I couldn't be bothered this morning," said Kelly, looking sheepish. "I didn't think it would matter, you know? Like, I was in the pool anyway and only my shoulders were out of the water. Besides, I usually tan really easily."

"It's worse in the pool sometimes—the water reflects all the sun's rays and bounces them back to you," Phil explained. His manner had changed back to his patient, teacherly persona. "But it doesn't look too bad. The skin isn't peeling yet, so you've caught it early. If you can get some pure aloe gel on it, that should really help."

"Really?"

"Yes…" Phil's eye strayed to the windowsill and he perked up. "Hey! Well, whaddya know? Look, there's an aloe plant there, in a pot!"

He got off the bed and went over to the window. Carefully, he broke off one of the plant's fleshy leaves and brought it back to the two girls. They watched as he squeezed the aloe leaf and a clear, pale green gel oozed out.

"Here... apply this to your skin," he said, handing the leaf to Kelly.

She took it doubtfully but after she had dabbed some aloe gel on her bare shoulders, she gave a sigh of relief.

"Ohhh... that feels much better already." She looked up at Phil with a teasing grin. "Thanks for that. You're my hero."

He reddened and looked down, shuffling his feet. "Uh... it was nothing."

"No, no, I think it was really clever," said Kelly. "I'm gonna remember that trick next time."

"You can also use it on normal burns. You know, like if you scald yourself while cooking—"

"Or baking," said Kelly with a wink. "So... you're a baker, huh? That's kinda a weird hobby for a young man, isn't it? Most guys I know are into, like, martial arts or biking or video games or something."

"Oh... uh... well, I... I do other stuff too. I don't just bake—"

"No, it's cool," said Kelly, grinning. "I've got a kinda weird hobby myself: I'm really into plushies."

"Oh, I like plushies too!" said Phil, his face brightening. "I still keep my old Care Bear next to the bed—" He broke off suddenly, blushing a fiery red.

"Uh... I mean... not that I sleep with it or anything—
"

"Omigod, you've got a Care Bear?" Kelly squealed. "Which one? I've been, like, trying to collect them, but they're so expensive now, especially the vintage ones. I've got two of the original ten, but the one that I'm really after is the 1984 Goodluck Care Bear. Which one have you got?"

"Tenderheart Bear," said Phil, blushing. "But... but like I said, I'm... I'm into other stuff too," he stammered. "Like... like manly stuff... Uh, so... how did you get into baking?" he asked Kelly, obviously ready to change the subject.

"Oh, I think I was just rebelling to begin with," said Kelly, giggling. "My parents are originally from Vietnam. Most of the desserts my mom made when I was growing up were, like, sago puddings and coconut jellies and glutinous rice cakes. But what *I* really wanted was stuff like chocolate chip cookies and apple pie, like all my friends were having at school. So I learned how to bake them myself." She gave an ironic laugh. "Of course, now that I'm all grown up, I kinda appreciate Vietnamese desserts much more, and I'm always begging my mom to teach me how to make them!"

"You're both making me feel very guilty," said Ellie with a wry smile. "I can't bake anything at all!"

They sat and talked for a little longer, but soon Ellie got up to leave. She could see that Phil was fine now, and besides, with Kelly keeping him company, she wasn't worried about leaving him alone. They seemed to have gotten back on the subject of plushies and Phil had overcome his shyness enough to confess to Kelly about his own collection of stuffed animals. She left them chatting animatedly and left the clinic. She was a bit sorry not to catch Blake on his return, but she knew she would run into him around the resort sooner or later. Besides, she wanted some time alone to think.

Ellie walked slowly back to the pool, feeling troubled. She knew that Phil could have been lying, but his explanations did sound reasonable, and he just seemed too "nice" to be a killer. Besides, he was right—her idea for his motive was just too ludicrous. So did that mean that Phil was out as a suspect? And what about Angela? If Ellie believed the woman's excuse for having antifreeze in her car and that her piping bag was innocent, then who else did that leave? Melanie? Kelly? Chef Marcel? Chad Coleman's mysterious wife? They were the only people around the ballroom that night who could have had either the opportunity or the motive.

Or both, in Chef Marcel's case, thought Ellie. She thought again of the Frenchman's weirdly aggressive reaction to her being in his freezer. What was he hiding in there? She wished there was some way she could sneak back into that freezer to check it again.

Ellie paused as she passed a large post with several signs pointing in different directions. The signs had labels saying things like: "Main Pool,"

"*Hammerheads Bar and Grill*," "Tennis Courts," and "Lobby"—but the one that made her stop was the sign which read "Spa." Ellie decided suddenly to go and find Aunt Olive, instead of heading back to the pool. She was eager to tell her aunt what Phil had said, and ask her opinion.

She set off in the direction that the "Spa" sign was pointing and soon reached a secluded courtyard with a fountain and lots of lush greenery. Ferns, begonias, and other tropical plants grew around the stepping-stone pathway, which led to a large building designed to look like a wooden hut. Inside, there was a calm, peaceful ambience and a soothing fragrance of lavender. Hidden speakers played the sound of ocean waves, mingled with a soft piano melody.

Ellie went up to the reception counter and was just about to ask the girl if her aunt had finished her treatment when the silence was broken by a shrill voice shouting:

"No! Not like that! Freakin' flamingos, haven't you ever done a manicure before? I might as well do it myself!"

A minute later, a woman stormed out of the inner rooms of the spa and came into the reception area. Ellie's eyes widened. It was the same woman she had seen coming out of Detective Carson's interview room, the same woman she was sure she'd seen on the night of the murder... it was Talisha Coleman, the murdered man's wife.

CHAPTER TWENTY

Ellie stared as Talisha Coleman marched up to the reception counter. The other woman ignored Ellie and didn't even bother to say "excuse me" as she pushed in front. She scowled at the receptionist and said:

"That manicurist is a moron! I'm not having her do my nails. I want a refund or I'm going to complain to Mr. Papadopoulos himself!"

"I'm sorry, Mrs. Coleman. We do have other nail technicians, if you would like to try—"

"Where's Chloe? She always used to do my nails."

"I'm afraid she went on maternity leave. But we do have many other excellent technicians—"

"That's what they told me when I booked! I'm not having some trainee butcher my nails again." Talisha Coleman glanced irritably at her watch. "Anyway, I don't have time for this. I gotta go. You've made me late for my lunch date already!"

"I'm sorry, Mrs. Coleman—"

"Yeah, yeah... whatever. I'll call later to rebook." Whirling in a dramatic manner, Talisha Coleman tossed back her dark hair and sashayed out of the spa.

"My goodness, what a bad-tempered cow!" came a familiar voice, and Ellie turned to see Aunt Olive coming out of the inner rooms of the spa. Her aunt was wearing a white terrycloth robe and had a towel turban on her head. Her face was pink and glowing, with a strangely slimy sheen. She came over to join Ellie at the counter and gave the receptionist a sympathetic smile.

"Personally, I think your therapists are wonderful," she told the girl.

"Oh, thank you, ma'am!" said the receptionist. "We do try our best to make our guests happy." She sighed. "But some are harder to please than others."

As they walked back to their villa, Ellie said to her aunt: "So... how was your facial?"

"Oh, fabulous, poppet! It's one of the spa's newest treatments. They put organically raised snails on your face—"

"*Snails?*"

"—yes, and they leave the snails to slime around for a bit. Then the therapist removes them and massages some snail mucus cream into your skin. It helps to repair damaged cells. You should really try it sometime."

"Ugh. No thanks," said Ellie hurriedly.

Aunt Olive gave her a severe look. "You'll regret it, dear, if you don't look after your skin. Do you want to end up wrinkled like a prune?"

"Well, no, but—"

"Then you need to follow a strict beauty regimen! Cold cream before bed, a flannel to scrub your face, a good soak in a bath with Epsom salts, used teabags on the eyes..." She thrust her face toward Ellie. "Look at me—can you tell that I'm sixty-four?"

Ellie had to admit that Aunt Olive had fabulous skin for her age. "Well, I'm happy to try your cold cream, but I'll skip the snail facial. I'm glad you enjoyed it, though."

"I would have enjoyed it more if *that woman* hadn't been so loud," said Aunt Olive, frowning. "My goodness, she never shut up! All I could hear was her voice every minute going 'Freakin' flamingos—this' and 'Freakin' flamingos—that.' I'm sure she put her poor therapist off—"

"Wait, Aunt Olive—what did you say?" interrupted Ellie suddenly. She frowned. "That phrase: *'freakin' flamingos'*... I thought it sounded familiar when I heard Talisha Coleman say it, but now that you're repeating it, I'm sure I've heard it before. But where?"

"Maybe it's a local Florida expression? Although I have to say, I haven't heard anyone use it. It's almost the kind of thing you expect a cartoon character to say. But then that woman *was* like a cartoon

140

character—a total caricature!" declared Aunt Olive. "You know, when I was a little girl, my mother used to say 'pretty is as pretty does'—and Talisha Coleman is a perfect example. She was very attractive until she opened her mouth. It was like listening to a screeching parrot—"

"*Parrot!* Of course, Hemingway!" cried Ellie. "That's where I heard the phrase before!"

"Pardon?" Aunt Olive looked at her quizzically.

"You know, Hemingway, the resort parrot. I ran into him yesterday and he kept repeating words which didn't make any sense to me at the time. One of them was '*freakin' flamingos.*'" Ellie paused thoughtfully. "Hmm... I wonder if Hemingway picked that up from Talisha Coleman? You know he's a great mimic and he's always copying things that guests say."

"I wouldn't be surprised. He'd just have to fly past her whenever she came to the resort and he'd hear her saying it a dozen times," said Aunt Olive. "I hope he didn't pick up anything else from her. That woman has a foul mouth."

"No, it was just a lot of gibberish—something about using your imagination and moon juice."

"Moon juice?"

"Yeah, he said..." Ellie furrowed her brow, trying to remember what the parrot had said. "Something like: '*Moon juice, are you crazy?*'"

"Are you sure he said '*moon juice*' and not something else?"

"Like what?"

"Well, like... like '*mon Dieu.*' That means 'my God' in French and it sounds quite similar."

Ellie stopped in her tracks and stared at her aunt. "Bloody hell, you're right! That could have been what Hemingway said. But do you know what that means, then? He could have been mimicking Chef Marcel!"

Aunt Olive looked surprised. "Why do you say that?"

"Don't you remember when we arrived at the kitchen last night for the Key lime pie lesson? Chef Marcel was yelling '*Mon Dieu... I will roast you like a pig*' as he chased Mojito out of the kitchen."

"But it's quite a common French expression," Aunt Olive reminded her. "It's just like 'my God' in English. Lots of people say it. Hemingway could have picked it up from anyone. There must be other French guests at the resort and the parrot could have learned the phrase from any of them."

"Yes, but Hemingway said it at the same time as that '*freakin' flamingos*' phrase. It was as if he learned them together. I'm sure the two things are connected!" Ellie insisted. "Maybe Talisha Coleman came to the resort to meet Chef Marcel on the night of the pie judging, and Hemingway overheard them talking. Maybe they were plotting together to murder Chad Coleman!"

"Aren't you rather jumping to conclusions, dear?" asked Aunt Olive. "That sounds like something from one of my novels."

"I thought you said art imitated life?"

"Well, art is *inspired* by life but—"

"I've got to find Hemingway," said Ellie. "I've got to get him to repeat the phrases again. Maybe he picked up more words."

"Well, not before lunch," said Aunt Olive firmly. "I've booked a table for us at a lovely place outside the resort. Sol recommended it, actually. He says it's a local institution and I promised him we'd go and try it out today."

An hour later, Ellie followed her aunt into a cafeteria-style restaurant buzzing with people, from local workers to families with children. The décor might have looked low-key but the menu was filled with delicious dishes from Cuban and Spanish cuisine, like *ropa vieja* and *arroz con leche*. Aunt Olive ordered roast pork with yellow rice and a side of *tostones*—fried plantain slices. Ellie decided to go for a *filet salteado*: a tender fillet steak sautéed with chorizo sausage, onions, green pepper, potatoes, garlic, and red wine, and served with yellow rice.

"Ahhh, this is one of the nicest things about Florida," said Aunt Olive, surveying her plate with a happy sigh as the food arrived. "There's such a diverse mix of cultures and you get such a variety of cuisines when you're eating out. Where else can you get authentic Latin food like this outside Central America?" She glanced around. "Oh, but we forgot to order drinks! How about sharing a pitcher of sangria, poppet? The resort car's coming to pick us up later so we don't have to worry about driving."

Ellie readily agreed and when the sangria came, she eagerly poured herself a glass. "Mmm... this is delicious! Although I'll bet it's really lethal," she added. "It's so sweet and fruity that you don't notice the alcohol."

"Oh, this is nothing," scoffed Aunt Olive. "I'll tell you what's really lethal: a vodka watermelon!"

"A vodka watermelon? You mean, like a cocktail made of vodka and watermelon juice?"

"No, no, poppet, I mean literally an entire watermelon infused with vodka," said Aunt Olive, chuckling. "It was a favorite at a lot of the parties I went to when I was a young woman. You just cut a hole in the rind of the watermelon and stick a bottle of vodka into it, upside down. Then you wait several hours—ideally overnight—and the vodka will have drained through the hole and infused into the melon flesh. Then you can cut up the watermelon and take it for picnics and such, and nobody will know how much vodka you're carting along." She winked at Ellie. "An excellent way to hide booze for a bit of underage drinking. Maybe I'll teach Karen's kids when they're older."

"Aunt Olive!" said Ellie. She knew that her aunt was outspoken and unconventional, but she was still scandalized sometimes to hear Aunt Olive say or do things that no senior person normally would.

They enjoyed a leisurely lunch and Ellie found the food so good that she stuffed herself silly. She felt so full afterwards, she could barely get up from the table. When they got back to the resort, she found it hard to muster up the energy to go searching for Hemingway. Instead, she gladly followed her aunt's suggestion and sprawled on a lounge chair by the pool, dozing in the dappled sunshine filtering down through the palm trees. She awoke a few hours later, just as the shadows were lengthening and the sun was starting to sink lower in the sky. Sitting up and stretching, Ellie decided that her nap had been useful after all: she felt refreshed and raring to go.

She set off searching for the scarlet macaw. First, she looked around the pool deck, especially by the palm trees near the Tiki Bar, where he liked to perch and watch the guests coming to order their cocktails. But there was not a red feather in sight. Next, she looked in the lobby, but the parrot was not on his stand in the corner. She tried the tennis courts, the kids' Pirate Playground, the mini-golf course, the gift shop... She even plowed across the sand dunes to the Snack Shack to see if the parrot was perched on one of the wooden barrels there. He wasn't, but on a hunch, she bought a small portion of the resort's famous spicy nut mix before she continued her search.

Finally, Ellie returned to the lobby in frustration. She walked back over to the large bird stand where Hemingway usually perched. *My goodness, parrots sure are messy,* she thought, looking at all the broken nut shells, splintered wood, pieces of fruit, and other rubbish littering the tray at the base of the stand. Attached to the wooden perch itself, there were various bird toys. Several had mirrors or bits of sparkling glass attached and Ellie remembered Blake telling her that Hemingway loved shiny things.

Maybe I should just leave my sunglasses as bait out in the middle of a lawn and wait for Hemingway to see them and swoop down to grab them, she thought wryly to herself.

Then she groped on top of her head. Wait... where *were* her sunglasses? Ellie looked around in alarm, patting her body, checking in her pockets. Her sunglasses were gone! She realized that they must have dropped off somewhere while she was wandering around the resort, looking for the parrot. Her heart sank at the thought of having to retrace her route, looking for her shades. She had gone to so many places and meandered all over the resort—how was she going to search everywhere that she'd been?

"Excuse me?" came a voice.

Ellie turned to find a familiar-looking woman standing next to her. For a moment, she had a hard time placing her; then as she took in the flowing tie-dye kaftan, the long bead necklaces, and the strange turban on the woman's head, she suddenly recognized her.

Oh no, thought Ellie. *It's that crazy woman from beach yoga. Is she going to tell me I'm standing in her place in the lobby now?*

But to her surprise, the woman said: "Are you OK?

You look like you've lost something."

"Yes, my sunglasses," said Ellie with a sigh. "I think I must have dropped them somewhere in the resort, but I don't know where! I've been all over the place this afternoon and I don't know how I'm going to search in all the spots I've been."

"What did they look like?" asked the woman.

"They were aviator shades—"

"With pink mirrored lenses?"

Ellie looked at her in surprise. "Yes, that's right! How did you know?"

"I found a pair of shades just like that," said the woman with a smile. "By the pool. I was walking past and I saw them on the ground next to one of the lounge chairs."

"Oh!" said Ellie. "I was by the pool earlier. I guess I must have dropped them there, actually, rather than when I was walking around."

"I turned them in to the Lost & Found," said the woman. "You should find them there." She pressed her palms together and bowed. "*Namaste.*"

"Oh, thank you!" said Ellie in surprised delight. "And... erm... *namaste*," she added hastily.

As she made her way to the Lost & Found office, Ellie felt slightly bad for maligning the woman earlier. *I guess you never know where a friendly hand might come from*, she reflected. She arrived at the office and found a harassed-looking resort staff member dealing with a large Chinese tour group, all of whom seem to have lost something but none of whom spoke any English. She waited patiently next to them for several minutes before the assistant gestured to the tourists to wait a moment and turned to her.

"Yes, ma'am?" he said.

"I'm looking for my shades. Someone told me they'd found them and dropped them in here."

"They might be back there," said the assistant, gesturing to a shelf behind the counter. "I'm sorry, I can't look for them at the moment." He grimaced as he glanced at the loudly arguing Chinese tourists again. "As you can see, I've got a bit of a situation here."

"Do you mind if I have a look myself?" asked Ellie. "They're very distinctive: aviator-style with pink mirrored shades."

"Uh... sure," said the assistant. He swung the flap on the counter open. "Help yourself."

Ellie stepped into the little room behind the counter and began searching through the shelf. It was piled high with various items that had obviously been turned in recently. She was amazed at the things that guests lost at a resort: from a pair of snakeskin designer high heels to a set of false teeth, from a breast pump (with some milk collected!) to a Chihuahua-sized tuxedo... Then, just as she was about to give up, she spotted her shades poking out from beneath a large plush toy.

Elated, Ellie lifted the toy and pounced on her sunglasses. She was just about to put the plush toy back on the shelf when something rolled out of a split seam in its side. Ellie frowned as she bent to pick the item up. She stared at the small citrus fruit: it was a Key lime.

CHAPTER TWENTY-ONE

"Erm... excuse me?" Ellie went up to the assistant, who was still struggling to communicate with the Chinese tourists. "Do you remember who turned this in?" She held up the plush toy for him to see.

The assistant rounded impatiently on her. "Are you kidding? People drop off dozens of things every day." Then he caught himself and gave her an apologetic look. "Sorry, ma'am. I'm having a bit of a bad day. Didn't mean to take it out on you."

"That's OK," said Ellie with a sympathetic smile.

The assistant took the plush toy from her and examined it for a moment. "Hmm... sorry, no, I can't seem to remember who brought it in. It wasn't anyone special, if you know what I mean. Like, no one that stood out." He paused, then added, "But I seem to remember that they said they'd found this by the pavilion."

"The pavilion where the Key Lime Pie Contest took place?" said Ellie eagerly.

"Yeah, that's the one. They said it was under a bush. It must have got kicked under there."

Ellie left the Lost & Found office a few minutes later, clutching the toy. The assistant had been distracted by the Chinese tour group again and it hadn't been very hard to convince him to let her have it, after she promised to bring it back if anyone should ask for it. Ellie looked down at the stuffed toy in her hand. It was designed to look like a cute seashell, she realized. It had the sort of half-moon shape of a clamshell, with a smiling face stitched on one side and a little gap where a clam would normally open its two shell halves. This was where the Key lime had fallen out, and as Ellie inserted her hand into the gap, she found that there was a little pocket in the center of the toy where things could be stored.

Or hidden, she thought. She stared down at the toy. *Was it just a coincidence that this toy should have been found near the contest pavilion?* Then she realized something else that was an odd coincidence. This clam plush toy with its smiling face reminded her of the little plush toys that Kelly had showed her when they were chatting by the Tiki Bar. One of those had been in the shape of a starfish but the other had been in the shape of a clam! *Coincidence again?*

Suddenly, Ellie heard Melanie's voice in her head again: "*Kelly's obsessed with plushies. She's got hundreds and hundreds of them, and she even brought one along to the contest as a sort of good-luck charm. She had it on her workstation with her."*

Ellie looked back down at the plush toy. *Is this Kelly's? Was this the 'mascot' she'd brought to the contest and conveniently placed on her workstation?* She looked thoughtfully at the Key lime in her other hand. She raised the small citrus fruit to eye level, examining it closer. She frowned in puzzlement. She could see tiny pinpricks on the surface of the lime— almost as if someone had been sticking pins in it.

What's that about? Ellie wondered. She felt like she had so many questions and no answers. Slowly, she walked back to the villa and made sure both her sunglasses and the plush toy were safely stowed in her suitcase. Her aunt had returned from the pool and was having a bath. She must have heard Ellie come in because she called out:

"Is that you, poppet? Where have you been?"

"I've been searching for Hemingway, although I can't find him anywhere," said Ellie, huffing with frustration as she walked into her aunt's en suite bathroom. She found Aunt Olive sitting in the tub, surrounded by steam and bubbles.

"The parrot? I saw him when I popped by the lobby on the way back to the villa," said Aunt Olive.

"But I checked the lobby! Twice! He wasn't there."

"Oh, he wasn't in the lobby—he was out the front," said Aunt Olive, massaging some gooey green mixture into her cheeks. "Apparently, he likes to perch on the fountain in the main driveway and watch the guests arriving. That's what the bellman told me."

Sure enough, when Ellie made her way back to the lobby and stepped out of the front entrance, she saw Hemingway instantly. There was a circular flowerbed in the middle of the main driveway, with a fountain in its center made of a marble dolphin rising from a pool of water. The scarlet macaw was perched on the dolphin's dorsal fin, busily preening his feathers.

Ellie glanced left and right to make sure that no car was coming, then crossed the driveway and climbed into the circular flowerbed.

"Hey Hemingway..." she said, holding a hand out to the bird.

The parrot raised his head and fixed her with his beady eye. For a moment, Ellie thought he might fly over to perch on her shoulder, but after studying her for a moment, Hemingway lost interest in her. He ducked his head under his wing again and continued preening his feathers.

Hmm. Time for reinforcements, thought Ellie. She dug her hand into her pocket and pulled out the little paper bag of spicy mixed nuts. Shaking some into her palm, she held this out to the macaw and said:

"Look, Hemingway! Look what I've brought for you..."

The parrot raised his head again and Ellie saw his pupils dilate as he saw the nuts. He hopped across the back of the dolphin so that he was closer to her and stretched out his neck.

"WANNA NUT?"

Ellie laughed. "Yes, you want a nut, Hemingway?"

The parrot bobbed up and down excitedly, and stretched his neck out again.

"OK, well, you have to work for it," said Ellie. She picked a large Brazil nut out of her palm and held it up for Hemingway to see. Then she said: "Freakin' flamingos! Freakin' flamingos!"

The parrot cocked his head and looked at her.

"Freakin' flamingos!" repeated Ellie, beginning to feel stupid. "Come on, Hemingway—remember that phrase? What else did you hear that night?"

Hemingway tilted his head the other way. Then he flapped his wings and gave an ear-splitting screech. "WANNA NUT? WANNA NUT?"

Ellie winced. She glanced quickly at the resort entrance, where a few guests were congregating. They were starting to whisper among themselves and point at her. Ellie took a deep breath and turned her back to them. She focused once more on the parrot.

"Come on, Hemingway," she said in a coaxing voice. "Can't you just repeat what you heard?"

"WANNA NUT?"

Ellie sighed. "All right. Here's one." She handed him the Brazil nut and watched as he cracked it happily with his beak. In a few seconds, it was gone and he extended a claw for another one.

"WANNA NUT?"

"No, this time you really have to earn it," said Ellie firmly. "Come on, Hemingway... freakin' flamingos! Remember? Freakin' flamingos!"

"FREAKIN' FLAMINGOS!"

"Yes!" said Ellie, handing him another nut. "Good boy! What else did they say?"

"FREAKIN' FLAMINGOS!" The parrot bobbed up and down. "FREAKIN' FLAMINGOS!"

"Yes, OK, but what else? Remember the other day? You said other stuff..." Ellie looked hopefully at the macaw.

But Hemingway was silent. Ellie sighed. This was probably a stupid idea anyway. She rose and was about to turn away when suddenly the parrot said:

"FREAKIN' FLAMINGOS! USE YOUR IMAGINATION!"

Ellie whirled back. "Yes! Yes, Hemingway, good boy!" She gave him a couple more nuts, then waited hopefully again.

Hemingway eyed the remaining nuts in her palm, then he wiggled his tail feathers and said: "FREAKIN' FLAMINGOS! USE YOUR IMAGINATION!" His voice changed and he added in a deeper tone: "MON DIEU, ARE YOU CRAZY?" He bobbed up and down. "MON DIEU, ARE YOU CRAZY? WHAT IF SOMEONE FINDS OUT?"

Ellie whooped. "Yes! Good boy, Hemingway, you did it!"

Seeing her excitement, the scarlet macaw began flapping his wings and screeching as well. He made so much noise that one of the bellmen ran over to them.

"Uh… is everything OK, ma'am?"

"Yes, yes, fine… sorry," said Ellie, calming down slightly. "I was just… erm… having some fun with Hemingway."

She poured the rest of the nuts in her palm onto the dolphin's snout, next to the parrot. Leaving Hemingway cracking nuts and making happy chattering noises to himself, Ellie hurried back into the resort. *I must tell Detective Carson*, she thought excitedly. *This could be the key to solving the mystery!* If Chef Marcel and Talisha Coleman had been conspiring together to murder Chad Coleman, then that put a totally different spin on the case.

Then she paused, frowning. She just realized that she had no proof. There was no record of Hemingway saying those phrases and she couldn't guarantee that she could get him to repeat everything again. Ellie cursed herself for not thinking of videoing the parrot. Without the footage, she had nothing to show the police, nothing to point the finger at Talisha Coleman and Chef Marcel…

Wait a minute! Ellie brightened as she suddenly remembered the mysterious package in the kitchen freezer. That could be the lead she needed. After all, why else would Marcel have acted so scared about her "snooping" in his freezer if he wasn't guilty?

Ellie set her lips. *I've got to get back in that freezer and see what's in that package.*

CHAPTER TWENTY-TWO

Ellie tiptoed out of her room and paused outside her aunt's bedroom door. She could hear the sound of soft snoring. Good, Aunt Olive was sound asleep. Carefully, she tiptoed down the corridor, across the living area, and past the kitchenette. As quietly as she could, she opened the front door of the villa and stepped outside.

Ellie paused for a moment, looking up and down the pathway in case there were other guests around, but she saw no one. It was past midnight and it looked like most guests were tucked up in their beds. Of course, this being a holiday resort, there might still be some people up, perhaps at the late-night bars or just hanging out in the lobby, so she would have to be careful.

Keeping to the shadows, Ellie hurried through

various courtyards and past several accommodation wings until she came to the main resort building. She knew that she would have to cross the lobby to get to the large corridor on the other side which led to the entrance of the display kitchen. She decided that the best thing was to act as casual and natural as possible. Taking a deep breath, she stepped through the rear doors leading into the lobby and began to stroll through.

In spite of the late hour, there were a few guests lounging on the couches in the seating area and a couple drinking at the lobby bar, but no one paid any attention to Ellie as she walked past. The reception counter was staffed by just one girl, who had her head down, busily typing on her keyboard. The only other sign of life was Mojito the resort cat, who was sitting on the reception counter grooming herself. She paused as she saw Ellie and twitched her tail inquiringly. Hastily, Ellie looked away, trying not to catch the animal's attention.

Ellie kept walking until she reached the other side of the lobby and paused just before turning the corner to glance back. Everyone was engrossed in their own business, and no one seemed to have noticed her—except for Mojito, who had jumped off the reception counter and was trotting after her. Ellie darted around the corner and breathed a sigh of relief as she finally reached the display kitchen window. It was darkened now, as the kitchen had been emptied and shut for the day. Ellie continued down the corridor to the door which led into the small anteroom outside the kitchen. But when she tried the handle, it wouldn't turn.

Bugger! Ellie thought. She had stupidly not even thought about how she would get into the kitchen. For some reason, she had just assumed that the doors would be unlocked. Now she wondered what to do. Short of picking the lock, there was no way she could get inside.

"*MIAOW!*"

Ellie looked up and smiled as she saw Mojito farther up the corridor. The sleek black cat strolled toward her and stopped to rub herself against Ellie's ankles.

"So you decided to follow me, eh?" said Ellie, crouching down beside the cat and stroking her silky fur. Mojito began purring loudly.

"I don't suppose you know a secret way into the kitchen?" Ellie asked jokingly.

"*MIAOW!*"

The cat suddenly broke free and trotted back to the display window. As Ellie watched, Mojito jumped up onto the ledge beneath the glass pane and walked daintily past the baskets of plastic geraniums until she reached the end of the ledge. There, she nosed at the wooden shutters that framed the window. A minute later, to Ellie's astonishment, the cat disappeared!

"Mojito? Where did you go?" Ellie sprang up and ran over to where she had last seen the cat. As she reached out toward the wooden shutter, it suddenly swung open slightly and Mojito poked her nose out.

"*MIAOW!*"

Ellie chuckled. "So *this* is how you're getting into the kitchen every time! I wonder if Chef Marcel knows?"

She leaned closer to examine the shutter. It was a real wooden window shutter, not a decorative reproduction, and it had been embedded into the wall around the glass pane. But the latch which held the shutter shut had rusted away and was now loose. A gentle push in the right direction forced the shutter open and showed a gap into the kitchen beyond.

Ellie eyed the opening speculatively. She could probably squeeze through. Thank goodness she was a fairly skinny, petite person! She glanced up the corridor. It was empty at the moment but if anyone came around the corner from the lobby, they would instantly see her. She would have to move fast.

Taking a deep breath, Ellie tested the ledge beneath the window, then heaved herself up on it. Trying to move as daintily as the cat had, she perched on the ledge and leaned in through the opening in the shutter. She felt the sides of the wooden frame press into her hip and heard the wood creak and groan. Sucking her stomach in as hard as she could, Ellie wriggled in farther and, a minute later, gasped with relief as she squeezed through the opening and fell onto the counter on the other side. Quickly, she turned and pushed the shutter closed again. Then she peeked out the display window: the corridor outside was still empty. No one had seen her Spider-Man act. *Whew.*

Turning back to the kitchen, Ellie slid off the counter and looked around. She reminded herself that the front section of the kitchen was visible through the display window, and therefore she could be seen there if anyone were to come into the corridor and walk past. So she had to be careful to keep out of that area. But thankfully the freezer was at the back, which was out of sight of the window.

Ellie made her way to the rear of the kitchen, past the chiller cabinet, which was glowing weirdly in the dark. She stopped in front of the large metal door of the freezer. She paused for a moment to listen. In the distance, she could faintly hear sounds from the lobby—the clink of glass, the murmur of conversation and the occasional burst of laughter— and closer in, she could hear the loud hum of the chiller cabinet motor next to her. But otherwise, everything was quiet.

Ellie pulled open the freezer door. She was met by a gust of cold air. Glancing around, she spied a roll of baking paper sitting on the counter nearby. She tore off a piece, folded it over several times, and wedged it under the freezer door to stop it from swinging shut. Then she took a deep breath and stepped inside.

The light in the freezer had come on automatically when the door was opened. Ellie took a moment to get her bearings. It was freezing and she wished that she had put something on over her T-shirt before she left the villa. Still, she didn't intend to be in here long. She went quickly across to the far corner and reached up for the bag of ice on the top shelf. Chef Marcel had obviously replaced it on the shelf and wedged it back even deeper. Ellie had to stand on tiptoe, and even then, it was quite hard to get a good grip. Her fingers kept slipping on the cold plastic. She was just debating whether she should go back out to the kitchen to get a stool when she heard a sound.

Ellie froze. She jerked her head around, staring at the freezer door propped slightly open by the wedge of baking paper. She couldn't see out into the kitchen. Was someone out there? She held her breath, straining to listen.

But everything was silent now. After a few tense moments, Ellie let her breath out and decided that it must have been her imagination. Her hands were freezing now and she was getting goosebumps all over. She just wanted to check out the mysterious package on the top shelf, then get out of there.

Ellie turned her attention back to the bag of ice. She was just reaching for it again when she heard another noise. She whirled around and saw a small furry shape standing at the open freezer door. It was Mojito.

"*MIAOW!*"

"Oh, it's you!" said Ellie, clutching her chest in relief. "Mojito, you're going to give me a heart attack one day!"

"*MIAOW!*" said the cat, bounding happily into the freezer. As she did so, her back foot kicked against the piece of folded baking paper wedged under the door and it came loose, flying away across the kitchen.

"No!" gasped Ellie, diving for the door.

But it was too late. By the time she got there, the freezer door had swung shut. It slammed into place with a hiss of the rubber seal around the door frame. The light in the freezer went out, plunging them into darkness.

CHAPTER TWENTY-THREE

"Nooo!" cried Ellie, pushing frantically against the freezer door. It wouldn't budge. She groped in the dark, feeling for a handle, Her fingers found a push knob and she pressed it frantically, but nothing happened. With a sinking heart, Ellie suddenly remembered Chef Marcel's words the day before about the faulty safety latch on the door. She'd thought that he was just making up a lame excuse to get her out of the freezer, but it looked like he'd been telling the truth—at last about that. She turned around, rubbing her arms and shivering.

"*MIAOW?*" came a voice in the darkness and Ellie felt something warm brush against her ankles.

"It's all your fault, Mojito!" Ellie muttered. "We're both going to freeze to death in here."

Still, in spite of her annoyance with the cat, she

was glad that Mojito was in here with her. The thought of being locked in alone, in the dark, was horrible. She reached down and picked the cat up, cuddling her close and grateful for the warmth of the furry body. As the cat purred against her chest, Ellie suddenly thought of her cellphone. She groped in her pockets, but they were empty. She realized that in her hurry to leave the villa, she must have left it by her bedside. *What an idiot!* she berated herself. Now what was she going to do?

There was only one option left. She would have to make a lot of noise to attract attention and get help. It would mean that she would probably also have to explain to the resort security guards why she had broken into the kitchen. Ellie grimaced at the thought. But she had no choice. The kitchen would probably not be used until the early hours of the morning, when the pastry chefs came in to start the baking for the day. That was still at least two to three hours away. She would freeze to death by that time!

Putting Mojito down again, Ellie turned back to the freezer door and began banging on it with her fists. She also yelled as loud as she could. But the thick metal door muffled the sounds so much that she wondered if anyone could hear. As she kept banging and shouting, and there was no response, Ellie began to feel genuinely scared.

What if no one comes? What if I'm really trapped in here all night?

Up until now, she had been dismayed and

annoyed, but overall, her investigation had still had a sense of adventure and make-believe. It was like watching an exciting action film where you felt thrilled and scared, but you weren't really worried because you knew that it wasn't real. Except now, Ellie realized that this was very real. This wasn't a movie—she was actually trapped in a freezer—and the prospect of nobody coming to rescue her was becoming very real too.

Ellie felt a wave of panic overwhelm her. She threw herself back on the door with a renewed frenzy of pounding and yelling. She grabbed a leg of frozen ham off a hook and smacked that against the door, causing it to vibrate with a ringing "BOOM! BOOM! BOOM!" Then, just when she was about to give up in despair, she heard a muffled voice on the other side of the door.

"Hello? Is anyone there?"

"Yes!" shrieked Ellie. "Help! I'm trapped in the freezer! Get me out!"

A moment later, the door swung open and Ellie staggered out into the warm, humid air, with Mojito at her heels. She stumbled and tripped. Strong arms caught hold of her, then she was being pressed against a solid male chest.

"Ellie?" Blake stared at her in surprise. "What the hell were you doing in there?"

Ellie shivered and rubbed her bare arms, stammering: "Thank goodness you came, Blake! I thought I was going to be stuck in there all night and freeze to death!"

"But why were you in there?" asked Blake again.

"It was Mojito." Ellie pointed to the cat who was sitting a few feet away from them, washing herself. "She kicked away the piece of paper I used to wedge the freezer door open and it slammed shut."

"Yes, but *why* were you in the freezer in the first place?"

Ellie hesitated, looking up into Blake's brown eyes. Could she trust him? Could she tell him everything? She still didn't know Blake Thornton that well, but somehow her gut told her that she could trust him. "It's a long story," she said with a sigh.

"Well, I'm not on call, so I've got all night," said Blake with a teasing look.

Ellie started to speak, then realized suddenly that she was still snuggled up against Blake's chest. Hastily, she pushed away from him, stepping back and flushing.

"Sorry... I didn't mean to... it's just that you're warm—I mean..." Ellie stammered, blushing even more as she realized how that sounded.

Blake grinned. "I'm happy to be of service. But maybe we ought to get out of here before the security guards find us and you have even more explaining to do. How about a drink at the lobby bar?"

"Oh, wait," said Ellie, suddenly remembering the package in the freezer. It was the reason for this whole fiasco. She wasn't going to leave without checking it out!

"There's something in the freezer that I need to look at first," she told Blake. She eyed him up and down. "In fact, can you help me?"

She took him back into the freezer and—after Blake had propped the door securely open with one of the stainless-steel kitchen stools—she showed him the top shelf with the mysterious package. Blake was well over six feet tall and reached the bag of ice easily. He lifted it out of the way and dragged out the bulky package behind it. Lifting it down, he held it out to Ellie, who eagerly unfolded the layers of plastic that it was wrapped in.

When it was finally open, Ellie stared in bewilderment at what the package contained.

"It's... It's just frozen pastry!" she said.

Blake looked puzzled. "What did you expect it to be?"

Ellie didn't answer. She lifted out the plastic packets containing flat, rolled-out pastry dough. "I don't understand. Why was it being hidden up there? Chef Marcel practically jumped down my throat when he saw me, and he yelled at me not to touch the package. Why?"

Blake looked even more confused now. "I'm sorry—Chef Marcel? What about him?"

Ellie carefully wrapped the pastry sheets up again and handed them back to Blake. "Can you put these back? Then let's get out of here and I'll tell you all about it."

Blake returned the package to its original place, stowed the bag of ice on the shelf in front of it, then they left the freezer and shut the door firmly behind them.

"*Whew!* I need a hot drink after that," said Blake. He glanced at Ellie. "How about some midnight hot chocolate?"

"Sounds wonderful," said Ellie, smiling.

Blake started toward the kitchen door. "Come on, let's go get the drinks, then you can tell me your 'long story.'"

CHAPTER TWENTY-FOUR

Ellie followed Blake gratefully through the lobby, out the rear doors, and into the humid night air. She took a deep breath, relishing the warm breeze that caressed her face. As they walked slowly through the various courtyards that led to the pool, Ellie thought the resort seemed eerily quiet. *Well, that's hardly surprising—it's nearly two in the morning after all*, she reminded herself.

When they arrived beside the pool, Blake gestured to a few daybeds in the distance and said: "Why don't you pick one of those and get comfortable? I'll be right back."

Ellie did as he suggested. The large round daybeds were luxurious affairs, with a circular mattress surrounded by plump cushions and half-covered by a domed canopy which gave a sense of intimate privacy. They were positioned at the edge of the pool deck, in the shadow of one of the resort buildings. Ellie picked one which faced out toward the beach and stretched out on the comfortable cushions with a sigh of pleasure.

It would be so easy to doze off here, she thought. Then the peace was broken by a loud:

"*MIAOW!*"

Ellie raised herself up on one elbow, then gave an incredulous laugh as she peered over the side of the daybed and saw Mojito the resort cat looking up at her.

"Now where did you pop up from?" said Ellie. She looked at the cat severely. "I hope you're sorry. You nearly got us frozen to death!"

"*MIAOW!*" said Mojito, not looking the least bit contrite. Without waiting for an invitation, she jumped up to join Ellie on the cushions.

"Hey!" said Ellie as the cat climbed into her lap and made herself comfortable. Mojito nuzzled Ellie's hand and, before Ellie realized it, she was dutifully stroking the cat's silky fur. A loud purring filled the air.

How on earth do cats always manage to arrange things exactly how they like it and get humans to do exactly what they want? thought Ellie with a mixture of amusement and exasperation.

She heard footsteps approaching and she looked up to see Blake with two steaming mugs of hot chocolate.

"Wow—where did you conjure those up from?"

asked Ellie, impressed.

"I've got a friend in Room Service," said Blake with a wink. He handed her a mug which was topped with whipped cream and a sprinkle of chocolate flakes.

"Mm-mmm..." said Ellie, drinking the rich, creamy chocolate. "I think this is the best hot chocolate I've ever tasted!"

Blake laughed. "You've got a bit of whipped cream on your nose," he said, his eyes twinkling.

"Oh!" Ellie lowered the mug, blushing as she wiped the tip of her nose with the back of her hand.

"*MIAOW?*" said Mojito, stretching her nose toward Ellie's mug and eying the whipped cream with interest.

Unable to resist those big green eyes, Ellie dabbed a bit of the whipped cream onto her pinkie finger and held it out to the cat, who licked it daintily. Ellie laughed at the feel of the raspy tongue on her fingertip.

"I think you've made a friend for life now," said Blake, chuckling as he watched them.

Ellie rolled her eyes. "This cat is always following me around and sneaking up on me at the worst moments! Although I have to say, I would never have got into the kitchen tonight if it wasn't for her. She showed me the way through the loose shutter by the display window."

"Oh—is that how you got in? I was wondering. You were lucky that I happened to be staying late at the clinic and walked back to the lobby through that corridor. I don't know if anyone else would have heard you otherwise."

"So how did *you* get in the kitchen?" asked Ellie curiously. "I tried the door and it was locked."

Blake patted his pocket. "I have a set of master keys for the main resort areas. It's handy in case there's a medical emergency and I need to get somewhere quickly. I won't have to always wait for the head of security."

"Well, that's good to know!" declared Ellie. "You might have just made a friend for life now too," she teased.

Blake raised a wicked eyebrow. "Anytime you want to go breaking and entering, count me in." Then he turned serious and said: "What were you doing in that kitchen, Ellie?"

Ellie took a deep breath and began telling him everything, starting with how Mr. Papadopoulos had enlisted her to help investigate the murder case, and going through her encounters with Angela, Phil, Melanie, Kelly, Talisha Coleman, and Chef Marcel. She also told him about Hemingway's newest phrases, and her theory about where the parrot had learned the words. Blake listened without comment, leaning back on the daybed cushions, with his long legs stretched in front of him.

"I just feel like there's something I'm missing," said Ellie in frustration as she finished. "I mean, what about all these extra weird details that don't make sense... like that package of frozen pastry in the freezer... and that plush toy I found with the Key lime in its inner pocket... and the meaning of the weird things that Hemingway repeated? I can't shake off the feeling that they're all related to the case somehow, but I just can't figure out how. It's as if there is a big fat clue staring me in the face but I just can't see it."

"Maybe it would help if you viewed the contest footage," suggested Blake.

"What contest footage?"

"The TV footage of the contest. They were planning to broadcast it, remember, as part of a PR campaign for the resort. The police have taken custody of the footage as evidence in their investigation. But I'm sure you could ask Mr. Papadopoulos to see a copy of the video files."

"That's a brilliant idea!" said Ellie, sitting up. "I could go over the whole day again, knowing what I know now, and maybe something will jog my memory. I mean, maybe I've been working on the wrong assumption all along. Like... I always thought that the murderer added the poison *after* all the pies had been baked and were on their way to the ballroom. It seemed to be the only window of opportunity. But what if that's not true? What if they added it during the baking itself?"

"It would be pretty difficult, though, with the TV cameras and a live audience watching the contestants all the time," Blake pointed out.

"But not all the time," Ellie argued. "Think about

it—even when you go to watch a concert or a ballet or something, you can never watch everyone on stage simultaneously, can you? You might look at some of the dancers on the right side, then your eyes move to the dancers on the other side... or you might watch some of the musicians playing at the front, then you watch the ones playing at the back. So it's possible for someone to do something when everyone's attention is focused somewhere else. Like, for example, when poor Betty was forced to stop and leave the competition. That caused quite a stir when they had to help her out of the pavilion, and I'll bet no one was paying any attention to the other contestants or Chef Marcel at that time."

"Right, that's a good point," said Blake. "But how would he or she have managed to get the poison there in the first place? From what I've heard, the resort provided all the ingredients for the pies."

"Yes, Phil told me that they weren't allowed to bring any of their own ingredients from home. In any case, Key lime pies have so few ingredients, it would be hard to 'hide' any extra things added. It's mainly graham crackers, eggs, condensed milk, and Key lime juice." Ellie leaned back on her hands, her brow furrowed in thought. "Well, you can't put poison in the eggs and it's hard to get it on the graham crackers. The Key lime juice is freshly squeezed from the fruits provided, so it's not as if they could use a bottle that's been spiked with ethylene glycol. So I guess that leaves the condensed milk, but that comes in sealed cans too, so—"

Blake burst out laughing. "You know what? You remind me of a terrier my grandfather used to have. He was an ornery little beast, this dog. He would never give up on anything. If you told him not to do something, that would just make him try harder!"

Ellie shot him a look. "Erm... I'll take that as a compliment?"

Blake grinned at her. "Oh, it was meant as one. I liked that dog—I admire that kind of single-mindedness and persistence." He settled back against the cushions, with his arms crossed behind his head, and looked up at the night sky.

"Look... can you see Pegasus up there?" He pointed at some stars in the sky.

Ellie tilted her head up to look. "What am I supposed to be seeing?"

"You know, the winged horse from Greek myths—"

"I know what Pegasus looks like but I don't see any winged horse up there," said Ellie, squinting at the night sky.

Blake leaned close. "There... see? There's his snout... and his wings... and his back legs... You just have to imagine a line joining the stars together."

"If I do that, all I see is a big square," said Ellie.

"Oh, yeah, that's a constellation in Pegasus known as the Great Square."

"Are you one of those night sky nerds?" asked Ellie with mock horror.

Blake gave a sheepish smile. "I suppose I am. But you know, the skies over Florida are wonderful this time of the year. Winter is peak star-gazing time. If you're interested, I could take you night-watching sometime. The visibility down on the beach is pretty awesome."

"That sounds lovely," said Ellie, suddenly conscious of how close Blake was.

Hastily, she turned her gaze to the sky, making a big show of peering at it intently. She tried to focus on the view above them, at the twinkling stars framed by palm trees on one side and one of the resort building on the other. Each room in the building had a wide balcony, and Ellie could see that the balcony closest to them had its windows open because of the warm night. The sheer white inner curtains billowed in the breeze coming off the sea, looking almost like ghostly shapes.

However, no matter how much she tried to keep her mind on these things, Ellie was still very conscious of Blake lying next to her. They weren't exactly touching, but there was still an intimacy in their similar positions, lying against the cushions, staring up at the sky together. There was no sound except for the faint rhythmic murmur of the waves in the distance and the occasional call of a seagull.

Ellie threw a surreptitious look at Blake and caught him looking at her in a way that made her heart begin to beat faster. *What would he do if I suddenly leaned over and kissed him?* she wondered.

Then she pulled herself up. *What am I thinking? The last thing I need right now is a holiday romance! I'm letting the seductive atmosphere of the beach and the balmy night air and the handsome man next to me go to my head,* she berated herself.

But Ellie couldn't stop other thoughts from entering her mind. *Didn't I want adventure in my life? Wasn't that why I came to Florida? I wanted change and new experiences and excitement. Well, what's more new and exciting than a vacation fling?*

Ellie stole another look at Blake and had the weirdest feeling that he had read her mind. She saw his eyes flicker to her lips and her pulse began to race. He moved slightly, leaning toward her. Ellie held her breath, vacillating between shifting back to keep the distance between them or leaning forward and meeting him halfway.

Then the silence was broken by a plaintive: "*MIAOOOOW!*"

Mojito sprang up from between them, flicking her tail and looking at Blake reproachfully. He shifted hastily, realizing that he had inadvertently leaned on the cat. Ellie jerked back and sat up, her cheeks hot. The spell was broken and she was slightly ashamed of what she had almost let happen.

"Erm... It's getting late. I should really get some sleep," she said, sliding off the daybed.

"Yes, of course," said Blake, clearing his throat and standing up as well. "I've got an early start tomorrow too. Uh... I'll walk you back to your room," he said rather formally.

They walked to Aunt Olive's villa in silence. Blake hesitated for a moment as they stood outside her front door, and then, with a quiet "Good night," he turned and disappeared down the path which led back to the main part of the resort.

Ellie let herself into the darkened villa and paused to listen for a moment after she shut the front door. Aunt Olive's soft snoring drifted out from her bedroom. *Whew.* At least she wouldn't have to explain where she'd been to her aunt. Ellie tiptoed back to her own room, undressed, then climbed into bed with a sigh.

It was good that nothing happened, she told herself firmly. No matter how sexy and charming he was, she shouldn't get involved with Blake. He was American and his life was here in Florida. Hers was back in London. This was just a fantasy: this luxury resort with the beautiful beach, the delicious exotic food, the quirky local residents... No matter how great a time she was having now, sooner or later, she would have to return to her real life in England. She was enjoying a vacation—no need to complicate things!

Still, as she drifted off to sleep, Ellie couldn't help imagining what it would have been like to feel Blake's lips, warm on hers...

CHAPTER TWENTY-FIVE

The next morning, Ellie rushed through breakfast. She was eager to visit the resort offices afterwards to ask to view the footage from the Key Lime Pie Contest.

"My goodness, poppet, you're going to give yourself indigestion if you eat that fast," said Aunt Olive, watching her disapprovingly. "It's important to chew your food thoroughly, you know. The Japanese are famous for being the longest-lived race in the world and they have an ancient philosophy which says that you should chew your food thirty times before swallowing."

"Yeah, that's why they live so long... because they need to finish chewing," muttered Ellie.

"Pardon?"

"Nothing, Aunt Olive," said Ellie, gulping down her

last mouthful of pancake. "I've chewed five times. I'll chew the other twenty-five on the way," she said, jumping up and giving her aunt a peck on the cheek before hurrying out of the dining room.

As she was stepping out of the restaurant, she bumped into Melanie also coming out as well.

"Hi!" she said. "I didn't realize that you were still here."

Melanie made a face. "I'm hoping the police might let us go home today. I mean, not that I don't love it here—the resort is fantastic—but I kinda want to go home and see my hubby."

Ellie gave her a sympathetic smile. "I'm sure you must miss your little boys too."

"Oh yeah... I've bought them both presents from the gift shop though. I can't wait to see their faces when they open them!"

"Did you get a replacement for the toy you lost?"

"Oh, no, I found that," said Melanie quickly. "I just wanted to get them something else. It's not super expensive or anything, but the boys won't mind. They'll just be excited that Mommy brought them gifts." She smiled.

"Where's Kelly, by the way?" asked Ellie, looking around.

Melanie frowned. "I dunno. She was supposed to meet me for breakfast, but she never showed up." She hesitated, then lowered her voice and said: "She's been acting kinda weird, actually."

"What do you mean?" said Ellie.

Melanie shrugged. "I don't know. Just kinda jumpy and distracted. Last night, we were having dinner together and talking about what happened at the contest, and Phil came up behind us. Well, Kelly just clammed up suddenly, like she was afraid he'd overheard her or something."

"What were you talking about?"

"Oh, you know, just what it was like on the day of the contest, how nervous we were and stuff. Kelly's workstation was next to Phil's and she was telling me she thought he was watching her out of the corner of his eye. That was when he came over to join us. Maybe she was embarrassed he overheard her or something."

Or maybe Kelly had been doing something to her pie that she hadn't wanted Phil—or anyone else—to see? wondered Ellie. She thought again of Kelly's hobby of collecting plush toys and the strange coincidence of the soft toy she had found, with the Key lime stashed in its inner pocket.

Melanie looked at her curiously. "You seem like you're in a big rush. Where are you off to?"

"Oh, just the lobby, actually. I... erm... I wanted to ask the manager something."

"I'll come with you," said Melanie. "I want to check the lobby to see if Kelly's around. I went over to her room late last night to ask if she wanted to grab a hot chocolate or something together, and she wasn't there. It was really late, almost midnight. I wonder where she went. And now she's missed breakfast. I hope she's OK."

They walked to the main resort building together and parted company as they entered the lobby. Ellie went up to the reception counter and asked if she could speak to the manager, Mr. Anderson. When the balding, middle-aged man came out from the inner offices, she explained her request.

"I'm sorry—what makes you think you can have access to the footage?" said Mr. Anderson suspiciously.

"Speak to Mr. Papadopoulos—he'll vouch for me," said Ellie.

A few minutes later, a slightly mollified Mr. Anderson came back out with a DVD disc in his hand. "Well, I've got to say, this all seems very strange to me, but Mr. Papadopoulos says you're kosher, and hey, he's the boss." He handed Ellie the disc. "Here, this is a copy of the footage that we gave to the police. You can watch it in one of the cubicles in the Business Center over there." He pointed to the other side of the lobby. "Please bring it back here when you're done."

Ellie followed his instructions, going over to the door marked "Business Center" on the other side of the lobby. She found a suite of plush offices inside, furnished with couches, small conference tables, individual computers, and outlets for those who wanted to use their own laptops. A couple of businessmen were talking on their phones and a woman in a smart suit was standing by the printer, collating documents.

Ellie made her way to one of the cubicles with a computer and slid her disc into the machine. There was a handy pair of earphones lying next to the screen and she put these on. Then she clicked on the first video file and began to watch.

For the next hour, Ellie slowly went through the footage. It was pretty tedious work, and she began to have more sympathy for police detectives who probably had to do this a lot of the time. And this was footage of an actual event! She couldn't imagine how boring footage from a surveillance camera in a street or building foyer must be.

She went through the videos in reverse, starting from the judging and Chad Coleman's collapse, and working backward through the day until she got to the start of the contest. She watched Coleman taste each pie and tried to discern any expression in the faces of the contestants which might betray their murderous intentions. She watched Chef Marcel bustle around the pavilion, shouting and looking important. She watched each of the contestants busily stirring, mixing, pouring, and pounding at their workstations. And she saw nothing: nothing new, nothing unusual, nothing remotely suspicious.

Ellie leaned back in her seat and blew out a sigh of frustration. Her eyes felt sore from staring at the screen and her neck ached. She felt like giving up. But there was one last video file left.

Come on, I've got to do the last one. Just for

completion, she told herself.

She clicked on it wearily and watched as Barbara Watts welcomed viewers to the contest and then began introducing each of the contestants. Then Ellie sat up straighter. *Wait... what was that?* She hit the mouse, clicking to pause the video, and stared at the blurry image on screen. It showed the corner of one of the workstations, and propped amongst all the ingredients and baking equipment was a plush toy in the shape of a smiling clamshell.

It looked identical to the one she had found—the one which had the Key lime in its inner pocket. Was this Kelly's "mascot"? Her thoughts racing, Ellie dragged the cursor back to replay the section again. She watched as the camera panned around to show the rest of the workstation and the young woman standing there, looking innocent and pretty in her simple cotton dress and apron.

It was Melanie Caruso.

CHAPTER TWENTY-SIX

Ellie stared at the screen in disbelief. Oh my God, could the murderer be... Melanie?

She rewound the section and watched it again. On the screen, Melanie was talking to Barbara and, as she answered questions, she was rummaging in a large diaper bag. It slipped suddenly from her fingers and fell open. Various items tumbled out: baby food, wet wipes, pacifiers, diapers... and a plush toy in the shape of a clamshell. Melanie hastily picked these items up and stacked them on the countertop of her workstation in a messy pile, then she straightened, embarrassed and apologetic. Her face was flushed, her manner flustered, as though she had rushed out of her house and grabbed her kids' diaper bag by mistake—just as she'd said. She looked like a typical suburban American mom... and the last person in the world who would commit a murder.

Which is exactly what she'd intended.

Ellie had been fooled just like everyone else. She had been there in the pavilion that day, yet she had hardly paid any attention to the items that had fallen out of the diaper bag and which Melanie had then stacked on her workstation. And as the contest continued, nobody else thought twice about the pile of kid's things at the end of Melanie's counter. She had explained the innocuous reason for having them there—put the items upfront for everyone to see— and then, after that, everyone had dismissed them. They had become part of the background. Which meant that when the audience's attention was distracted by one of the other contestants, Melanie could have easily slipped the poison out of the pile and added it to her pie with nobody noticing.

But wait... Ellie frowned. In this case, the thing Melanie had obviously slipped out were the Key limes that had been hidden in the inner pocket of the clamshell plush toy. She had used the juice from those in her pie, instead of the ones provided by the resort. That implied that the Key limes contained the poison in some way. But how? They weren't like a bottle of Key lime juice to which ethylene glycol could easily be added. These were whole fruit which couldn't be tampered with.

Or could they?

Ellie sat up excitedly. She suddenly remembered those mysterious pinpricks in the skin of the Key lime she'd found in the plush toy. She'd assumed that someone had stuck pins into the small citrus fruit and it had been a complete mystery to her why they would have done that. But what if it hadn't been pins that had been inserted into the fruit—what if it had been syringe needles?

Yes! That was how it had been done! Just like the vodka-spiked watermelon that Aunt Olive had mentioned. But rather than inserting a bottle of vodka into a hole cut into a melon, this was on a microscopic scale. Melanie had painstakingly injected ethylene glycol via a syringe into several Key limes, causing their juices to become infused with the deadly poison. Then she simply had to juice them and use them in the recipe as normal, and there was no risk of anyone seeing her add something "unusual" during her baking. Ellie remembered excitedly that Chad Coleman had complained about one pie tasting excessively sweet—this explained it!

The only hard part for Melanie was getting her poisoned Key limes onto her workstation in the first place. And she had achieved that with a clever trick using classic misdirection. Once they were in place, camouflaged by all the baby paraphernalia, Melanie had grabbed them from inside of the plush toy and quickly transferred them to the top of her bowl of fruit when everyone else's attention was elsewhere. Then she just had to make sure that she only used Key limes from the top of the bowl—which is what most people would have done anyway. Nothing suspicious there. That had been the beauty and cleverness of Melanie's ploy: she could add poison to her pie in broad daylight, under everyone's noses, and no one would even notice, much less suspect. It was ingenious.

I've got to get that Key lime that I found in the plush toy tested, thought Ellie. If I'm right, they'll find that it's full of ethylene glycol. It must have been a leftover one which Melanie missed. Together with this footage, it will tie the "murder weapon" to Melanie and be enough for the police to arrest her and question her.

Because Ellie still didn't know why. One reason she had never seriously suspected Melanie was because the young housewife seemed to have no connection to Chad Coleman, no motive to want to kill him. Now Ellie tried to think back over things that Melanie had said, and she realized suddenly that she hardly knew anything about the woman's background. Melanie had given the impression of being friendly and chatty, but had actually revealed very little about herself. Ellie knew she had a husband who "worked so hard" and she vaguely remembered that he was a chef who used to have his own restaurant. The fact that he was now working in a diner suggested that the restaurant business had failed... Did Chad Coleman have something to do with that?

Quickly, Ellie opened up a browser and tried to search for a restaurant connected to the name

"Caruso." It was a common Italian surname and America was a big place, but after some cross-referencing against Coleman's name and the area of Georgia where Melanie had said she came from, Ellie finally hit the jackpot. It was a small article in a local paper, written by Chad Coleman, which included a scathing review of a newly opened family restaurant:

"Nonna Caruso's Trattoria is supposed to be just like your Italian grandma's kitchen. It's supposed to offer familiar Italian favorites, dished up in a homely atmosphere. Well, in a word... it sucks. The food is bland and boring, the staff is clueless, and the décor is cheap and cheesy. If I want to eat crappy, home-cooked food, I can get it for free in my own grandmother's kitchen. I'm certainly not going to haul myself out to this place and pay through the nose for it! My best advice to you is: avoid this dump!"

Ellie did some more searching, this time looking for the restaurant by name, and she came across a small notice in a business news site which listed Nonna Caruso's Trattoria as closed and filing for bankruptcy. The date was not long after Coleman's review. It seemed that after the influential food critic had given his verdict, no one had been willing to give the fledgling restaurant a chance.

Ellie leaned back in her chair with a sigh. It was all coming together now. Melanie did have the perfect motive after all. What better reason for murder than to punish the man who had destroyed her husband's dream and forced the family business into bankruptcy?

I've got to tell the police all this! thought Ellie excitedly.

She shut down the files and ejected the disc, then stood up and was just about to turn around and leave the cubicle when there was a sudden movement behind her.

Ellie froze as she felt a sharp blade press into the soft flesh at the back of her neck.

CHAPTER TWENTY-SEVEN

"I was wondering when you would figure it out," said Melanie's voice beside Ellie's ear. "When I heard you talking last night with that hunky doctor, outside my window—"

"Oh my God, that was your window?" gasped Ellie, suddenly remembering the balcony with the open windows and the flimsy white curtains billowing in the sea breeze.

"Yup, I was right on top of you, listening to every word. Lucky for me, huh? When I heard you mention finding that stupid toy and the Key lime hidden inside, and then talk about viewing the footage, I knew it wouldn't take you long to put two and two together. So I made sure I got to breakfast really early this morning so that I could keep an eye on you and your aunt. And when you got up to leave, I made sure

I followed you." Melanie's voice sounded smug. "How did you like the way I engineered 'bumping into' you just as you were leaving the dining room?"

"So that was all fake?" asked Ellie. "Everything you said was just lies?"

"Not everything. I really don't know where that dumb cow Kelly went last night, and she really has been acting kinda weird recently—but the rest? Yeah, that was all made up. All of it: the happy families, everything."

"You mean..." Suddenly it dawned on Ellie. "You don't really have kids, do you? That's why you acted a bit confused every time I asked about them. Oh, you recovered really well—you sure know how to think on your feet! Like, you quickly covered up with that lie about buying them toys from the gift shop. But it was a slip-up."

"Yeah, well, nobody's perfect."

"You did it twice: first when I mentioned that your boys must be really disappointed that you didn't win, and the second time when I said they must be missing you. You looked startled both times, before you recovered yourself. It had been vaguely bothering me, although I didn't know why. Now I know: they were just props, weren't they? Because what could be more innocent and unthreatening than a young mother with toddlers?"

"Well, look at you—Little Miss Nancy Drew," said Melanie in a sneering tone. "You've got it all worked out, haven't you?"

"Yes, and I've worked out why you did it too," said Ellie. "It was because Chad Coleman gave your husband's restaurant a bad review, wasn't it?"

"He never gave us a chance!" snarled Melanie, jolted at last out of playing cool. "My husband Tony, he put everything into that restaurant. His 'nonna' was an amazing woman and he always dreamt of having a place that would share his grandmother's recipes with the world. But we had some teething problems in the first year. What new business doesn't? And then Chad Coleman came and gave us *that* review…"

Melanie's voice turned bitter. "Things just went downhill from there. And it was all Coleman's fault. He had no compassion, no heart—he didn't cut us some slack and give us a chance. No, he completely destroyed us. And he enjoyed it too! That was what made me decide that he had to pay. Giving a bad review is one thing, but he enjoyed trashing us, grinding us under his heel. So as soon as I saw the ad for the Key Lime Pie Contest, with Coleman as the judge, I knew that my chance had come. I started planning. I knew exactly how to play it. After all, who would ever suspect a sweet soccer mom from the Ol' South?" she said.

"I did," said Ellie.

"Yeah, well, no one's gonna find out what you know by the time I finish with you."

"You… you can't do anything to me," said Ellie, licking her lips nervously. "We're in the middle of a busy resort."

Melanie laughed. "Just watch me."

"I'll scream for help!"

The knife blade pressed deeper into Ellie's skin, making her flinch. Then it moved with agonizing slowness over her shoulders, down her spine, and out under her ribs until it was pressing against the right side of her lower back.

"Don't even think about it," said Melanie softly. "If you scream or do anything stupid, my knife will go straight in and slice through your liver. There are a lot of blood vessels in the liver—*a lot*. You'd lose enough blood to die in minutes, d'you understand me?"

Ellie gulped and gave a slight nod.

"Good. Now come on!" Melanie grabbed Ellie and jerked her around. "We're going to walk out of here, nice and easy, and you're going to smile and look like you're just strolling along with a girlfriend."

Ellie looked wildly around as they stepped out of the cubicle. She was still hoping that there might be someone around that she could signal for help. But the Business Center was empty. All the guests who had been in there earlier had left.

"Where are you taking me?" asked Ellie as they stepped out of the Business Center together.

"Oh, I'll think of somewhere." Melanie giggled. "You know, the good thing about Florida is that it's full of ponds and waterways, usually with a nice fat alligator. No one is going to think twice if your body washes up on some bank in a couple of days, with some bits chopped away. They'll just think that you're yet another poor tourist who was the victim of a 'gator attack."

The words were chilling and Ellie tried not to let panic fill her as they walked slowly through the lobby and out the rear doors. Melanie walked beside her, with one arm slung across Ellie's shoulders, pulling her close, and the other arm tucked between them, so that no one could see the knife jabbing into Ellie's side. They probably looked like two "besties" strolling through the resort. Ellie's heart sank. How was she ever going to get away?

CHAPTER TWENTY-EIGHT

They stepped outside and Ellie was instantly engulfed by the hot, humid air. The sun was blazing down; it was going to be a roasting day. She couldn't believe that there were so many people within shouting distance, but with every step, she could feel the point of the knife *jab-jab-jabbing* against her side, and she didn't dare risk calling for help.

"Where are you taking me?" she asked again.

"Just keep quiet and keep walking," said Melanie, jabbing the knife harder.

They walked down the pathways and through the courtyards between the various resort buildings, until they reached the wide walkway which led past the pool. A smaller path branched off from this main walkway and Ellie remembered that this led to the parking lot where she had helped Angela with her suitcase. She guessed that that was where Melanie was taking her. Perhaps the other woman had a car parked there. Ellie swallowed. She knew that once she got into Melanie's car, she was done for. She had to find a way to get help while she was still here in the resort.

Then she caught sight of a flash of red feathers above her head and her heart skipped a beat. *Of course! Hemingway!*

She looked up. The parrot was perched on a palm tree nearby, nibbling something in one claw. Ellie took a deep breath. It was a long shot, but it was worth a try. Carefully, she reached into her pocket.

"Keep your hands where I can see them," snapped Melanie.

"I'm just getting my sunglasses," said Ellie. "The sun is hurting my eyes."

Before the other woman could protest, she fished her aviator shades out of her pocket and put them on. Then she raised her face up and tilted it this way and that, trying to let the sun reflect off the pink mirrored lenses as much as possible. They sparkled and flashed like a disco ball.

Hemingway froze, staring. He gave a loud squawk and took off. A second later, he swooped down toward them, flapping his enormous wings and screeching with excitement.

Melanie cried out and stumbled backward. The minute Ellie felt the sharp tip of the knife withdraw from her skin, she whirled around. Snatching the sunglasses off her face, she flung them in Melanie's direction.

Hemingway gave another ear-piercing screech and turned in mid-flight. He swooped toward the other woman, his claws extended.

"Get away! Get away from me!" screamed Melanie, waving her arms in a panic.

She dropped the knife with a clatter. Ellie jumped forward and kicked it out of reach. It shot into some bushes nearby and disappeared.

"Aaarrghh! Help!" yelled Melanie, trying to run away from Hemingway.

"FREAKIN' FLAMINGOS!" screeched Hemingway.

Ellie couldn't help it. She burst out laughing. It was so ridiculous that it was like something out of a farce. She clutched her stomach, laughing so hard that she started to hiccup, as she watched Hemingway grab her sunglasses, pivot in mid-air, then flap away, screeching triumphantly. He left Melanie in a huddle in the middle of the walkway, her arms over her head, moaning: "Go away! Go away!"

A crowd was starting to gather. People started to rush toward Melanie in concern.

"What happened?"

"Did you see? That parrot attacked a woman!"

"Someone should report it to the manager."

"No, Hemingway's really sweet! He would never hurt anyone."

"I saw it with my own eyes! He dive-bombed her!"

Mr. Papadopoulos suddenly pushed his way out

of the crowd and hurried over to Melanie. His face was a mask of horror and concern.

"My goodness, Mrs. Caruso—are you all right? What happened? I can't believe... Hemingway has never been known to attack without provocation—"

"That bird is a menace! He should be shot!" someone yelled.

"No!" said Ellie loudly. She stepped forward. "On the contrary, you should give Hemingway a medal."

"What? Why?" several people demanded.

"Because he saved my life," said Ellie, looking around at all of them. "And he helped to apprehend a criminal."

Mr. Papadopoulos looked astounded. "A criminal! What do you mean?"

Ellie pointed to Melanie. "This is Chad Coleman's murderer."

CHAPTER TWENTY-NINE

"Great gibbons, Melanie is the murderer?" Aunt Olive looked horrified. "I can't believe I didn't figure that out! I should have known! I'm a mystery author—I'm supposed to have the nostrils for these things."

She looked so crestfallen that Ellie said quickly, "But you were the one who first suspected that Chad Coleman's death was murder, remember? Even before the police started an investigation."

"Ah yes, that's right," said Aunt Olive, perking up.

"There's something I still can't figure out though," said Ellie with a frown. "That mysterious package in Chef Marcel's freezer... what does that have to do with anything? Was it not connected to the murder at all? In which case, why did he act so guilty about it?"

"You said you opened it, dear—what was in it?"

"Nothing special. Just a bunch of ready-made pastry sheets."

Aunt Olive's eyes gleamed. "When you say 'ready-made,' do you mean store-bought?"

"Erm... yeah, I think so," said Ellie, furrowing her brow as she tried to remember. "Yeah, they were in these plastic sleeves with printed logos."

"Ah... well, then, I think you have the answer to your mystery," said Aunt Olive with a smile. As Ellie continued to look blank, she said: "If you go on the resort's website and read the sections about Dining, there's a lot of fuss made about all the food— *especially the baking*—being handmade from scratch." She smirked. "However, it sounds like Chef Marcel is resorting to using some ready-made pastry! That would be a scandal if it were ever found out, which is why he reacted so badly. He was probably worried you would expose his secret."

"Really?" said Ellie skeptically. "Who cares if the pastry is ready-made?"

"It's a big deal in professional culinary circles," said Aunt Olive. "It's like turning up to a baking contest with a cake that you bought at the supermarket."

At that moment, Mr. Papadopoulos appeared in the lobby and hurried across to join them.

"Mrs. Goldberg, your niece has truly been amazing," he said, looking warmly at Ellie. "I knew I was right to put my faith in her!"

Ellie blushed. "Well, some of it was luck, really—"

"Oh no," said Aunt Olive, wagging a finger. "Luck has nothing to do with it, poppet. Persistence, resourcefulness, and keeping an open mind—that's what makes a good sleuth."

Mr. Papadopoulos laughed. "As I said before… listen to your aunt, young lady. She's a bestselling mystery author; she knows what she's talking about when it comes to playing detective!"

"I hope you've given Hemingway a big bowl of mixed nuts for his contribution," said Ellie, smiling. "He literally saved my life yesterday. Actually, I thought he also provided me with some important clues by repeating something he'd overheard. But it turned out that they were nothing to do with the murder after all." Ellie frowned. "I still wish I could make sense of the words, though, and figure out what it was all about."

"Oh, is this the '*freakin' flamingos*' thing?" asked Aunt Olive. "When you thought Hemingway had overheard Chef Marcel and Talisha Coleman talking?"

"I'm *still* convinced that it was them talking outside the ballroom on the night of the murder!" said Ellie. "I thought they were plotting together to murder Chad Coleman, but that's obviously not the case. But they were definitely up to something." She sighed in frustration. "I just wish I knew what it was."

"Ah." Mr. Papadopoulos gave a small smile. "I might be able to help with that. Chef Marcel came to me this morning and confessed everything. He had been feeling guilty and uneasy, and even though the murderer has been arrested, he still wanted to make a clean breast of it." He looked at Ellie. "You were right, my dear. Chef Marcel and Talisha *did* meet outside the ballroom that night. And they *were* plotting together against Chad Coleman."

Ellie's eyes widened. "They were?"

Mr. Papadopoulos nodded. "Yes, but not murder. Talisha wanted Marcel to add some ground-up laxative to the pies, so that Coleman would be embarrassed on stage in front of the TV cameras and the live audience. She'd just found out that he was having an affair—*again*—and she was feeling angry and humiliated."

"Why should Chef Marcel help her? Were *they* lovers?" asked Aunt Olive eagerly. "Was he secretly in love with her all these years?"

Mr. Papadopoulos gave an apologetic laugh. "No, nothing quite so melodramatic, I'm afraid, Mrs. Goldberg. They were just good friends. They'd gotten to know each other very well when Coleman and Marcel were still running that restaurant together. They share a lot of similar hobbies and interests, and have remained friendly over the years despite the rift between the two men. In this case, however, Marcel refused to do it—"

"And Hemingway overheard the two of them arguing!" said Ellie. "That's what those phrases mean: Talisha must have been impatiently telling

Marcel to *'use your imagination'* to figure out a way to get the laxative on the pies. But he replied by saying: *'Are you crazy? What if someone finds out?'* Yes, it all makes sense now!"

"Well, I'm glad I've been able to solve part of the mystery for you," said Mr. Papadopoulos with a smile. "And now—"

He broke off as they heard a loud commotion coming from the reception counter. They turned to see Angela Brewer surrounded by Mr. Anderson the manager and a group of resort staff. The woman was gesticulating angrily and saying in a shrill voice:

"...I should have won! I know Chad Coleman was going to announce my name before he collapsed. I always win this contest every year—I'm the best baker here and everyone knows it! I want an honorary award. I'm telling you, I always win it every year and I can't have a gap on my shelf..."

Mr. Papadopoulos sighed and gave Ellie and her aunt an apologetic smile. "Excuse me, ladies. It appears that I have to go and help my manager resolve a situation."

They watched him walk reluctantly over to the group by the reception counter.

"What a pain that woman is," declared Aunt Olive, shooting Angela a withering look. "Really, they should ban her from entering the contest ever again!"

They left the lobby and strolled slowly back toward the rear of the resort, where the main pool was situated. On the way, they passed the colonnade which housed the miniature shopping strip, serving the resort guests. There was a small art gallery, a jeweler's, a hairdresser, a boutique selling designer shoes and handbags, and—at the end of the strip— the large gift shop selling souvenirs, merchandise, and beach paraphernalia.

"Shall we have a look in the jeweler?" suggested Aunt Olive. "I wanted to show you a pearl brooch I saw the other day which—"

She broke off as they saw Dolores Garcia hurrying toward them from the other side of the colonnade.

"Hello, Mrs. Garcia. I didn't realize you were still here," said Aunt Olive pleasantly.

"Oh, hi," said Dolores distractedly. "Actually, we're supposed to be leaving the resort soon. The manager is very kind and has organized a car for us. But I can't find Phil anywhere! He wasn't in his room so I thought he might have gone down to the lobby first to check out, but he wasn't there either. Have you seen him?"

"No—at least, not this morning."

Dolores clicked her tongue in frustration. "I don't know what's gotten into him lately! He never used to be like this. But he's been acting so strangely the last two days. He's distant and distracted..."

Ellie looked up. Suddenly, she remembered someone else who had been described the same way.

"Mrs. Garcia, when did Phil start behaving differently?" she asked.

The older woman thought a moment. "I think it

was ever since that afternoon when he hurt his back during a sneezing fit. He came back from the doctor's clinic and he was in the strangest mood. He seemed... well, happy and excited. He kept smiling to himself and I even heard him singing in the shower!"

"I've got a hunch... I think I might know why Phil is behaving so strangely," said Ellie, chuckling. "Hang on a minute—I'll be right back!"

She hurried to the end of the colonnade where the gift shop was and peered through the large display window. She scanned the interior of the shop, looking in particular at the far corner. Just as she remembered, there was a display of children's books and toys there, including a small mountain of plush toys in the shape of various sea animals. There were colorful clownfish, playful dolphins, fluffy pelicans, gangly octopuses... and standing in front of the pile was a couple with their heads together. They had their backs to Ellie but from the silky black hair on the girl and the slightly hunched posture of the man, she could easily guess their identities. They were deep in discussion over two sea turtle soft toys held in their hands and seemed oblivious to everything else around them.

Ellie turned and beckoned to Dolores and Aunt Olive. The two older women came over to join her.

"Look..." said Ellie, pointing through the windowpane.

"That's Phil? With a girl?" said Dolores, staring in delight.

"With a lovely girl called Kelly. She was one of the fellow contestants in the Key Lime Pie Contest," Ellie told her. She turned to her aunt. "And that's solved the last little mystery, Aunt Olive. Kelly had also been described as acting weird the last few days— distracted and disappearing at odd times. She had come into the clinic when Phil was there. In fact, I left them chatting together. I remember thinking, as I was leaving the clinic, how well they seemed to be getting on. I could hear them talking and laughing as if they'd known each other for years."

Aunt Olive chuckled as she looked at the couple in the shop. Their heads were so close together that there was no doubting the intimacy in their body language. "Phil might not have won the contest, but it looks like he found the real prize."

Ellie glanced again at the couple and grinned. "Yes, it looks like a match made in plushie heaven!"

CHAPTER THIRTY

"Well! What would you like to do today, poppet?" asked Aunt Olive as they left Dolores at the colonnade and continued on their way. "I thought you might like to do a bit of sightseeing for a change? We could go up to Clearwater Beach and check out the aquarium... or maybe do a daytrip to Busch Gardens... or how about the Dalí Museum? Now that all the mysteries have been wrapped up, there's no need to remain at the resort is there?"

"No, but..." Ellie hoped she wasn't blushing. "I've got a... erm... sort of date."

Aunt Olive's eyes gleamed. "Ooh! Not with the hunky young doctor?"

"Hush! Someone might hear you!" hissed Ellie, glancing quickly around.

Aunt Olive laughed. "I'm sure I'm not the first one

to call Blake Thornton that." She looked at her niece eagerly. "So where is he taking you? Somewhere romantic for dinner?"

"Erm... no, actually, we're meeting at the pool. He's helping me learn to swim."

Aunt Olive's face fell. "Learn to swim? What kind of a date is that?"

"Well, I don't really want it to be a date," said Ellie quickly. "I don't want things getting too romantic between me and Blake."

Aunt Olive looked astonished. "Why not?"

"Because... because it would be a vacation romance! And things could get complicated when I have to return to England."

Aunt Olive waved a dismissive hand. "Oh, that's still weeks away! Why worry about it now?"

"Because it would be silly to start something that could go nowhere."

Aunt Olive rolled her eyes. "Oh, for goodness' sake... doesn't your generation know how to have a fling? Who says every relationship has to go somewhere? If you're both footloose and fancy-free... and you enjoy each other's company, what's wrong with just having fun for now?"

Aunt Olive's words were still ringing in her head as Ellie made her way to the pool to meet Blake an hour later. She found him already doing laps and she stood for a moment, admiring the way he cut powerfully through the water. He saw her as he neared her side of the pool and swam over. He pulled himself out at the edge, water streaming from his muscled torso.

"Hey..." He smiled at her. "Ready for some water action?"

Ellie nodded nervously. "Just so you know, I can't float," she said quickly. "So I only stay where my feet can touch the bottom. And I've tried holding my breath under water, but something always goes wrong and I get water up my nose. And I've tried kicking and circling my arms, like I see other people doing, but I just keep sinking! And I don't—"

"Whoa... whoa!" said Blake, laughing. He put a gentle hand on Ellie's arm. "Relax. I'm not going to throw you in the water or anything. We'll go at your pace and we won't do anything that you're not comfortable with, OK?"

Ellie nodded nervously again, although she did feel slightly reassured by his words. She dropped her things on a nearby lounge chair and shimmied out of her sundress. Then—trying not to feel self-conscious in her bikini—she followed Blake around the pool to the side where wide, shallow steps led down into the water. He went in first, then turned around and waited patiently as Ellie slowly descended the steps. The water was lovely—cool and silky against her skin—and Ellie felt herself relax even more.

It's such a nice day, she thought, glancing up at the blue sky overhead. *The sun is shining, it's warm and balmy, and I'm at a beautiful beach resort with a gorgeous man for company...* Really, you couldn't find a nicer way to learn how to swim!

Taking a deep breath, she stretched out her arms and waded out to where Blake was waiting for her.

"OK, what do I do first?" she asked.

"Well... why don't we teach you how to float?" Blake suggested. "If you're not worried about sinking all the time, you might feel less scared in the water."

"I've tried," said Ellie. "I saw all these people floating on their backs and it looked so effortless, so I tried to do it too—but I just couldn't stay on top of the water! I kept sinking and when I tried to kick, I just sank even faster! Look, I'll show you..."

She lay back in the water and demonstrated, thrashing around for a few seconds before Blake caught her and helped her upright again. The sound of raucous laughter came from above, and when Ellie looked up, she saw Hemingway perched on a lounge chair next to the pool, watching them. The scarlet macaw was bobbing his head up and down, and mimicking a loud belly laugh.

"*HA HA HA HA HA! A-HA HA HA HA HA!*"

Ellie scowled at him. "What's so funny?"

The parrot cackled again, then yelled: "*GET BACK IN THE KIDDIE POOL!*"

"Oh, go away," Ellie grumbled, turning her back on the parrot.

"I think you're trying too hard," Blake said gently. "Floating doesn't mean that you have to be like a plank right on top of the water, you know. As long as you keep your head and chest above water, it doesn't matter if your legs are slightly lower. You just nee[d] to relax and breathe normally—the air in your lung[s] will keep you buoyant. Also, you only need a fe[w] gentle kicks to keep your legs up. Kicking too har[d] and too wildly just tires you out and makes you panic." He gave her an encouraging smile. "Look, why don't you try again, but this time you can lay back against my chest... Don't worry, I'll be right behind you and I'll hold you up if you start to sink, OK? Just try and let your body relax."

"OK," said Ellie doubtfully.

She took a deep breath and leaned slowly back into the water again. This time, she felt Blake's hard chest against her shoulders, supporting her. His arms came gently around her from behind, cradling her in the water. She felt safe. A sense of peace stole over her. Slowly, she let her arms and legs relax, and allowed her body to settle into the water. To her surprise, instead of sinking, she felt the water buoying her up.

"Oh my God! I'm floating! *I'm floating!*" she squealed, flailing her arms and legs in sudden excitement.

"Wait—Ellie, don't—careful!"

The next minute, Ellie went under. Water rushed into her eyes and nose and mouth. She choked and spluttered. Then she felt strong arms grab her and pull her up. Her head broke the surface. She blinked water out of her eyes, clutching at the first thing she could find, while from somewhere nearby came emingway's voice again:

"*HA HA HA HA HA! A-HA HA HA HA HA!*"

"Ellie... Ellie, are you all right?"

She looked up to see Blake regarding her with concern. "Erm... yeah, I think so," she said, coughing. "I think I swallowed a gallon of pool water, though," she added with a rueful smile.

Blake laughed. "We've all been there. Don't worry—a bit of chlorine won't hurt you."

Ellie realized suddenly that she had her arms around his neck and was clinging to him like a limpet. The water splashed and rippled around their bodies, emphasizing how close they were. She could feel Blake's breath warm on her face and she caught her own breath as she saw the look in his eyes. Her heart hammered in her chest, so fiercely that she was sure he could feel it.

Blake leaned slightly toward her, then hesitated, waiting for her to meet him halfway. Ellie stared up at him, wanting to but scared as well...

A loud, exaggerated kissing sound filled the air around them. Then Hemingway croaked: "KISSY... KISSY... KISSY!"

Ellie jerked back, flushing, just as Blake let go too. There was an awkward silence, which was broken only by Hemingway making that dreadful kissing sound again. Ellie shot the parrot a dirty look. She really wanted to throttle that bird sometimes!

Blake cleared his throat. "Uh... so... d'you want to try again? The floating I mean," he added hastily, his cheeks reddening.

"Yes," said Ellie quickly, trying to pretend that she hadn't heard the second part.

Glad to have something to do to ease the awkward moment, Ellie flung herself into the floating position. She found, to her delight, that this time it was even easier to relax into the water. She forgot about Hemingway and the embarrassing incident as she felt herself bobbing on the surface of the pool. She wriggled her fingers and kicked her legs gently, feeling them glide through the water. Then she let her feet sink, tipping her back upright, and stood up again as her toes touched the bottom.

"I did it!" she said jubilantly, beaming at Blake. She'd never felt such a wonderful sense of achievement.

"Yeah, you were awesome!" agreed Blake. "Everything's going to be easier now, you'll see."

"Yes, I don't feel so scared of the water anymore," said Ellie. She gave a little bounce in the water. "I can't wait to learn more! OK, what shall we do now?"

"Well..." Blake glanced at Hemingway, then turned back to her, his brown eyes twinkling. He moved slowly toward her. "You know what? I'd hate to disappoint the parrot..."

THE END

ABOUT THE AUTHOR

USA Today bestselling author H.Y. Hanna writes fun cozy mysteries filled with clever puzzles, lots of humor, quirky characters - and cats with big personalities! She is known for bringing wonderful settings to life, whether it's the historic city of Oxford, the beautiful English Cotswolds or the sunny beaches of coastal Florida.

After graduating from Oxford University, Hsin-Yi tried her hand at a variety of jobs, including advertising, modelling, teaching English, dog training and marketing... before returning to her first love: writing. She worked as a freelance writer for several years and has won awards for her novels, poetry, short stories and journalism.

A globe-trotter all her life, Hsin-Yi has lived in a variety of cultures, from Dubai to Auckland, London to New Jersey, but is now happily settled in Perth, Western Australia, with her husband and a rescue kitty named Muesli. You can learn more about her and her books at: www.hyhanna.com.: www.hyhanna.com

Join her Readers' Club Newsletter to get updates on new releases, exclusive giveaways and other book news!
https://www.hyhanna.com/newsletter

ACKNOWLEDGEMENTS

Once again, I am so grateful to my beta readers, Kathleen Costa and Connie Leap, for their help in giving me insights into American culture, habits and ways of speaking—as well as their wisdom, warm support and much-needed dose of common sense! I'm also so lucky to have an editor who used to work in a Florida beach resort in his youth, which means I get the benefit of someone with first-hand knowledge and experience of the setting to check the details.

And of course, to my husband, who is always there, listening patiently while I agonize over plot holes and offering tireless encouragement when I get the "writers' blues". I couldn't do it without him.

Made in United States
Orlando, FL
18 June 2023

34277007R00139